THE MIND FIELD

THE SCIENCE OFFICER: VOLUME 2

BLAZE WARD

KNOTTED ROAD PRESS

The Mind Field
Volume 2
Blaze Ward
Copyright © 2015 Blaze Ward
All rights reserved
Published by Knotted Road Press
www.KnottedRoadPress.com

ISBN: 978-1-64470-019-8

Cover art: Copyright © Innovari | Dreamstime.com - Spaceship And Asteroid Field Photo

Cover and interior design copyright © 2015 Knotted Road Press

Never miss a release!
If you'd like to be notified of new releases, sign up for my newsletter.

I only send out newsletters once a quarter, will never spam you, or use your email for nefarious purposes. You can also unsubscribe at any time.

http://www.blazeward.com/newsletter/

The Doomsday Vault

The Last Flagship

The Hammerfield Gambit

The Hammerfield Payoff

Doyle Iwakuma Stories

The Librarian

Demigod

Greater Than The Gods Intended

Other Science Fiction Stories

Myrmidons

Moonshot

Menelaus

Earthquake Gun

Moscow Gold

Fairchild

White Crane

***The Collective* Universe**

The Shipwrecked Mermaid

Imposters

BOOK THREE: MINEFIELD

PART ONE

It had started with a tea mug. The best stories usually did. Javier had learned that over the years. There was just something so prosaic, so utterly mundane, and yet so completely irrational about a good tea mug. Wars had probably been fought because of them.

He had certainly considered it.

He had, however, been willing to compromise. Eventually. By declaring victory.

It had been a hard fought contest.

It would begin as always. Javier would be midway through a cup of really good tea, at just the right temperature and strength, and he would set his mug down. Within moments, as if by magic, it would disappear.

At first, he had suspected pixies. Certainly, they would have accompanied mankind into space. And a pirate ship like *Storm Gauntlet* was almost certain to be completely infested with them. Everybody knew they were irresistibly drawn to pirates.

The truth, when it revealed itself, was even worse.

The pixies had minions.

There were several of them, as a matter of fact, carefully disguised as stewards and yeomen from the ship's mess and Officer's Wardroom.

They stalked Javier, wherever he went, stealing half-empty tea mugs.

After moments of panic induced by lack of caffeine, he would confront one of them.

"Where did my tea go?" he would invariably ask.

Those foul, treacherous minions would look at him, all innocent and things. "Oh, was that your tea, sir? Sorry. Would you like me to get you another?"

It had gone beyond a game with them. It had devolved into a full-scale, multi-front war that threatened to involve the whole crew and bring down the wrath of the Captain and the tea gods.

That is, until Javier visualized victory.

He saw it in a vision, like Galahad dreaming of The Grail. He pursued it secretly, obsessively, fanatically. He made offerings to the tea gods, and any lesser deities with whom he might curry favor. He was absolutely non-denominational in this sort of thing.

Until, finally, he achieved Greatness. Completion. Grailhood.

Javier looked down at his new tea mug and savored the first sips of victory.

Bribes paid to the machinists had yielded a hollow cylinder, slate gray, out of a hull-grade alloy that was a near-perfect insulator of heat and pretty much indestructible with any weapon Javier could hold in one hand. Not that he hadn't considered trying. You know, for science and stuff.

Other bribes had led him to Kianoush, a plain and somewhat average-looking woman who worked for the Purser as a logistics tech during the day, while she pursued visions of art in enamel and silver wire in her private time.

She had been a hard sell, a woman with no particular interests in fresh fruit or beautifully cooked repasts that showed his amazing skill programming a culinary-bot. She was, however, a sucker for a good story, especially one that involved evil pixies and stolen tea mugs. And she was willing to trade her work for good stories and occasional reference answers culled from Javier's many years of solitary space-faring and survey work.

From her, he had procured the artwork. Even a little Strike Corvette like *Storm Gauntlet* had a ship's crest, usually only seen in a small logo painted on the wall in the captain's cabin, as well as on the rarely-worn dress uniforms some of the officers maintained.

They were pirates, after all. Spit and polish was not at the top of the list of things. That was usually eating, followed closely by things with guns. Or maybe it was the other way around.

But she had taken that logo, that artistic heart of this thing that was the *Storm Gauntlet*, and engraved it into that mug, using magic he could not fathom without asking the reference computer, and then filled that etching with real, honest to Creator silver, poured while molten, or dipped. He couldn't remember. One of those. Absolutely.

Above it, a name to strike fear into civilians and pulp writers everywhere. *Storm Gauntlet*. A private-service, freelance Strike Corvette, retired from *Concord* Fleet service after the Great Wars were over and making ends meet with transportation gigs and occasional strong-arm jobs. Like the piracy that had cost him his own lovely little probe-cutter, *Mielikki*, and turned him, through twists and forays, into an officer aboard her.

Some days, he considered explaining to the crew what the term *janissary* meant, but usually decided it wasn't worth the effort. These people were entirely unliterary, to boot.

But he had his mug. And it had the ship's name and logo. Almost complete victory, since it was most certainly one of a kind, at least until some enterprising engineer with access to a power lathe and a CNC laser decided to start mass-producing them.

And they would.

No, he was already several steps ahead of that unfortunate bastard, whoever he might be. Below the logo, that was where the victory lay.

On one side, also etched and filled with silver, his name in bold, block letters. JAVIER ARITZA. Also a name for the pulp writers to make famous. Someday. Hopefully.

On the other side, that thing that would most certainly defeat the evil pixies and their dread minions. A title that was utterly unique in pirateness. One guaranteed to convey to them that this mug was not empty and abandoned, just waiting for them to take it away and clean when he wasn't looking. No, it was meant to be here, with him, for him. Like a candle in a window on a cold and stormy night, marking the path home.

THE SCIENCE OFFICER.

Plus, it would make a really nice memento, one of these days, when he finally managed to escape this ship and these people, and have them all hung from the highest yardarm he could find.

PART TWO

Javier was first into the conference room today. He needed time and space to spread out the implements of his tea ceremony on the desk. If others were there, he would have had to elbow people out of the way. Plus, it would have taken forever.

Captain Sokolov was known for fast meetings. Javier could imagine getting his tea perfect just as everyone else left the room. No, far better to have the tea ready, bracing him with warmth and caffeine, as the meeting started. He had, after all, transported those very tea plants from the Homeworld itself into space, and halfway across the damned galaxy.

Just because these pirates had made him a slave and cut up *Mielikki* was no reason to give up tea.

And she was still there, at least in spirit. The entire agricultural section of his little probe-cutter had been removed from her corpse like a plum's pit and stowed forward in *Storm Gauntlet*'s huge cargo bay. He didn't get to eat all the fresh fruit and vegetables himself, anymore, but obviously, he had to sample everything before passing it on the Wardroom. You know, quality control. That included tea leaves. His tea leaves. *The kind I'll cut you over, pal.*

So he took over one whole wing of the conference table and committed theater. And tea.

First, the screen was removed from the travel case and unfolded to mark his territory. Pirates tended to be territorial about their tables. Best to set the rules early.

This one was a bamboo frame with cloth stretched over it. Twenty-four centimeters tall and forty-eight long, it perfectly framed the piece of cloth he put down to keep things from sliding. Also so the cleaning crew stopped complaining about water rings and stains.

The portable brazier stood station in one corner. He powered it up and rested the cast iron pot atop it. Freshly distilled water from his personal stores went into the pot to heat. And heating it this way took forever. That was why he invariably ended up staying late after meetings.

The tea caddy came out of the case next, a lovely little canister he had found on some fringe world that had actually been made of bronze. *Who worked in bronze anymore, when you could mine asteroids for the really exotic shit?*

The whisk, the scoop, the cleaning bowl took their places. Javier lovingly cleaned each piece, just as he had putting them away. You never knew what crew member might get their cooties all over things when he wasn't looking. Especially the pixies.

And now, boiling.

Javier scooped his tea into the big industrial tea mug bearing his awesomeness, added just the right amount of water, and whisked it to textbook froth.

Perfection.

The ceremony felt incomplete without someone to hand

it to for appreciation. But he was surrounded by pirates. And Philistines.

"There better not be a candle heating that, Aritza," a voice said behind him. A deep, rich voice, attached to an average-looking man with a shaved head and a salt-and-pepper Vandyke.

Javier looked up at Captain Zakhar Sokolov and sighed dramatically. "Battery-powered, captain," he replied in a sing-song voice. This wasn't the first time they had had this conversation. "Engineering built it for me. I'm no longer allowed to play with fire aboard this ship."

"I'm just afraid you'll hurt yourself, Javier," he smiled evilly, "and then where would my investment in you be?"

Javier fixed him with his best stink-eye, but the Captain was apparently immune.

Two others entered right behind the captain. They took seats well away from Javier, as he had intended. The male, Piet Alferdinck, was the ship's Navigator. All Javier knew about him was that he was a quiet, competent professional, who apparently went back to his cabin when he was off duty and read. Javier had never asked what.

He understood the need to escape people and have private time. His was down in the botany bay, raising plants and tending his chickens. They were still better company than the crew. And they kept pixies at bay, like mirrors that blocked demons at doors.

The female was another story.

Two point one meters tall. Muscles on muscles, in places Javier wasn't even sure he had muscles. Above-average looking. She'd be kinda pretty if she ever smiled. If she even knew how. Bright green eyes and freckles. Brown hair buzzed close on both sides and spiked on top. Javier could see nine earrings in the ear facing him. He knew there were seven more on the other side.

It wasn't that he didn't like the *Storm Gauntlet's* Dragoon. He respected her as a violent professional who wasn't just a sociopath, but an experienced and competent sociopath. It was just that Djamila Sykora always seemed to have it in for him.

Granted, she hadn't bounced him off a bulkhead, intentionally, in at least seven months. Close combat training drills in the gym didn't count.

He still owed her.

Javier wasn't sure if she was going to be the first one up against the wall on that day, or the last.

But he smiled. She had at least made a visible effort not to antagonize him. Much. They were more like teenage siblings, now. He supposed he could live with that. Until the time came.

"Okay, people," the captain announced. "Short meeting and then to work."

Javier smiled. Just as his tea had achieved perfection. He could even leave with them today, although he might take the time to clean everything extra, just so they left first and left him alone.

"Two jumps will put us in our target system," the Captain said, bringing up a holographic projector. A small yellow-red star was off-center, with the big purple dot that represented *Storm Gauntlet* coming in from the other focus of a giant ellipse.

"We will come out of jump, do a quick scan of the area, and then move in towards the second planet." He read off a string of galactic coordinates that would have blown right by most people.

Javier had spent too many years doing survey work. The destination sounded familiar, but he couldn't place it.

"Captain," he said querulously, "does this system have a name?"

Sokolov returned the stink-eye from earlier. He did it better.

Fortunately, Javier was immune as well.

"It does," he said after a moment. "*A'Nacia.*"

Javier knew better than to say the first thing that came to mind, or the first profanity. *Are you insane?* was a given with these folks. That didn't stop him from thinking it. Loudly.

"Uh huh," Javier replied, sucking on his teeth and lower lip. He took a long sip of tea as the other three people in the room turned and stared at him.

"What?" he said finally. They were really starting to mess with his *wa* this morning. Uncool.

"I would have expected more of a reply, Aritza," Sokolov said with his head cocked. "Surely you, of all people, have an opinion. You always do."

Javier scowled sourly back at him, and then shrugged. "If you want to raid a haunted graveyard, there's not a lot I can do at this point to change your mind."

Sykora gave him an especially exasperated look today. She was all spit-and-polish commando bad-ass. In her eyes, Javier was constantly in and out of insubordination. Sometimes, she reminded him of his first ex-wife. The green eyes didn't help.

"Lady," Javier said, forestalling her whole argument, "the captain talked himself into it. He can talk himself out of it. Not like you people ever listen to me, anyway."

She arched an eyebrow at him anyway. It was a lovely eyebrow. She really wasn't that bad looking, if you liked amazons. Javier would still have to be even more drunk than her to consider it.

He sat back and sipped his tea instead.

Sykora turned to the Captain instead. "Haunted, sir?" she asked politely.

"Old sailor's tale, Sykora," the captain replied. "One of

the last battles of the Unification Wars was fought over *A'Nacia*. It was a terrible affair. *Pyrrhic*. One of those famous last stands for the last of the holdouts against the *Union of Man*."

"I see," she said. "*Neu Berne* does not cover that particular event, apparently."

Javier resisted snorting out loud.

Neu Berne had started the next round of warfare after that, the one that led to the breakup of the *Union of Man*, the Great Wars that only ended eighty-some years ago. *Neu Berne, The Union*, and *Balustrade* had all pretty much wiped each other out in the process, leaving the *Concord* as the only large political entity left to pick up the pieces. It had inherited galactic hegemony, almost by accident. At least it was far less of an imperialistic power than the others had been.

"So why do you think it's haunted, Javier?" Piet asked suddenly.

Javier blinked. He had forgotten the man was there, he tended to be so quiet.

"Ships that go there disappear, never to be heard from again," Javier shrugged. "Plus, major battlefield, with something like five separate national fleets destroyed there. Lots of ghosts around."

Javier turned to the Captain. "Why?"

Sokolov put on his Captain face, all the charm that reminded people he was in charge. Serious charisma.

"Because we're better armed than the average raider that goes in there," he began. "We're also going to be really sneaky about this, a lesson I learned from Aritza. And we have a Science Officer who's going to keep the ghosts and bad guys away."

Javier snorted, "I can't even keep pixies at bay."

"I beg your pardon?" Sokolov's whole face turned confused.

"Never mind," Javier replied. Pirates, and Philistines. All of them.

PART THREE

Captain Zakhar Sokolov sat quietly in his command chair and drank coffee from his battered tin mug. He had seen Aritza's custom-made cup, and considered having it copied, but thought better of it.

Aritza needed something to make him feel like he had some control over his life. Since being captured nearly a year ago, he had managed to carve out a niche for himself as a member of *Storm Gauntlet*'s crew. He was well respected, generally liked, and several people, including his chief ground combat officer, Sykora, owed him their lives.

Zakhar refrained from reminding her of that. Touchy, touchy subject.

But Javier also brought a brightness to the bridge, even if he was mostly a complete goofball. He was a competent goofball when he wanted to be. Right now, he needed to be.

Zakhar was mildly surprised at how well the Science Officer was handling the current operation. He had been expecting a running commentary of rude remarks from that corner of the bridge instead of silence. Perhaps he should turn on a microphone nearby and see if the man was muttering them under his breath. Perhaps later. No good would come of it now.

The Navigator, Piet, called the countdown. "Emergence in fifteen seconds," his voice rang out. This was the only time the man was loud. Other times, he was as quiet as Aritza was loud.

Right now, everybody was quiet. Zakhar wondered if Javier had been telling them ghost stories. It was something he would do.

Storm Gauntlet fell back into real space with a lurch that even the gravplates couldn't forestall. Something about the change in physics between universes occurring faster than the machinery could compensate for.

Zakhar settled himself back in his chair. So far, nobody heaving their guts up into a handy trashcan. It happened occasionally, more inner ear and psychology than bio-medical.

"Navigation," Zakhar called regally, "bring the engines on line and ahead slow."

"Belay that order," Javier snarled from his station.

Zakhar jumped as far out of his seat as his belt would allow.

"Nobody do nothin'," Javier continued savagely.

"Aritza," Sokolov barked, "explain yourself. This is my bridge."

"Yes, is it," Javier agreed without looking up from his console screen. One hand snaked out and touched a blue light flashing madly on his console. "And somebody out there just lit us up with a nice, solid weapon lock."

"Have they challenged us?" Zakhar asked, much less angry.

"Not yet," Javier replied. "Or rather, if they have, it wasn't on any of the standard channels."

"Where would it be?" asked the Gunner. Her hands were poised on her controls, but she was waiting patiently.

Javier looked over, fixed her dark eyes with one beady eye of his own. "Whatever you do, Mary-Elizabeth Suzuki, do not deploy turrets or open a launch bay," he said, deadly serious.

Zakhar was surprised. He didn't think Javier did deadly serious.

This must be really bad.

"All hands," Zakhar said, reinforcing the point and letting the bridge computer transmit the message ship-wide, "stand down. We have a situation outside the ship we are investigating."

He closed the channel and looked as his Science Officer. It already felt like one of those days where he was going to owe the man big again. How would they keep him aboard once he paid off his debts and was free?

"Javier," he asked, "what's your theory?"

Javier looked both ways, as if double-checking that nobody was about to do anything. He started to say something when a sudden chime on his console got his attention.

Zakhar felt the emotional lurch as Javier turned back to his screens instead of speaking. The whole bridge seemed to sag, waiting.

He watched Javier pull an earpiece and stick it in. The man listened for a few moments, shook his head, and muttered something under his breath so profane even Sokolov blinked.

"I found their transmission," Javier announced. "It's in Bulgarian, down on one of the lower, older channels hardly anybody uses anymore. That's the good news."

"What's the bad news?" Zakhar asked conversationally.

"It's an automated sentry challenge," he replied.

Zakhar used the same word Javier just had.

Mary-Elizabeth cocked her head at the two men. "Could you two explain that for the mere mortals around here?" she asked with a sarcastic edge that sounded remarkably like what Javier would have used. Obviously, the man was rubbing off on her. The professionalism would be good, but not the attitude problem.

Javier turned to Zakhar and raised an eyebrow.

"You found it, Javier," the Captain said. "You explain it. Do we know if it works?"

"No," Javier blew out a breath. "The only way to know that is when it fires, or fails to. I could live the rest of my days without knowing, thank you."

"Talk, mister," Mary-Elizabeth barked. "I'm getting tired of you yammering. Gimme data."

"Yeah, yeah. Fine."

Javier pushed a button on his console and the main screen suddenly showed a schematic of the local area. *Storm Gauntlet's* purple star sat in the middle, surrounded by other stars of various colors.

"We just jumped into a live minefield," he announced sourly. "I am beginning to map things based on their own signals, while not generating any of our own. Fortunately, we came in dark. The minefield is intelligent, but not fully sentient. It isn't sure if we're a newly arrived asteroid that just wandered into range, or an enemy starship it should kill. On channel 392, it is asking us for the correct authentication code to safely transit the kill zone."

Zakhar watched him pick up his mug and empty it in one go. It was going to be that kind of day.

"Why would sentience be bad, Javier?" Mary-Elizabeth asked.

"Because it would probably just shoot us anyway, Suzuki," Zakhar answered before Javier could.

"Oh," she said quietly. "Can it kill us?"

"Shields were down for the jump," Javier said. "Powering them up most assuredly triggers something, somewhere. There were dreadnaughts at the battle of *A'Nacia*, so there are probably guns big enough here to gig us like a frog."

"Gig?" someone asked from over near the engineering seats.

"The term our Science Officer is looking for is *splatter*," Zakhar replied. "That's a much more accurate, technical term. Boom."

"Recommendation, Captain?" Javier asked politely.

This day was turning into an absolute surprise as other sides of Aritza's behavior came out for the first time.

"Go ahead," Zakhar replied. Internally, he noted how much the two of them sounded like old *Concord* Fleet officers, which they were. The piracy veneer apparently wasn't that deep, after all.

"Can we start shutting down systems? Turn the air temp down so we have longer before we have to dump heat? Power off things that might accidentally generate a signal outside the ship? That sort of thing?"

Zakhar considered it. All things that made sense, since nobody knew what might trigger a lethal surprise. They might not know until it killed them, and then only for a few seconds.

"Agreed," he said. He keyed the general comm live. "Engineering, Bridge. We're going to start powering down some systems to run quieter. Please coordinate with the Science Officer. And tell people to dress warm."

"Yes, Captain," came the polite, diffident voice of Andreea Dalca, the Engineer.

Zakhar looked around the bridge. Command decision time. "Everybody shut down your stations and drop down to emergency crew only. The rest of you are still on duty, so go do paperwork or something."

Zakhar counted ten seconds until the only people on the bridge were himself, Aritza, and Sykora, the Dragoon. He didn't say anything to her. She was going to stay and keep a watch on everything the Science Officer did. At least she had stopped wearing a sidearm on the bridge. Most of the time.

The room went dim as Aritza brought the lights lower. Conserving power now meant conserving heat. He was going to need to grab a jacket out of his day cabin in a bit, but he had enough layers for now.

"Okay, hotshot," Zakhar said to the back of Aritza's head, "how do we get out of this one?"

"I promise you, Captain," Javier turned to look at him, "you will be the second one to know."

PART FOUR

DJAMILA WAS USED to complex multi-tasking. It was practically a requirement to be successful at what she did.

She could, for example, track two different moving targets and fire accurately at both, pistols in both hands and one eyeball following each. She was capable of zero-gravity maneuvers that had earned her the nickname *Ballerina of Death* from her teammates, back in her days with the *Neu Berne* Navy.

Right now, she was flexing individual muscles in her legs to keep them warm and loose, while she sat quietly at a dark console on the bridge and knitted. It gave the hands something to do while the legs worked. The mind was watching Javier Aritza, their much-vaunted Science Officer with his custom coffee cup, pace around a three dimensional projection of the local environment.

When asked, he had explained that pacing made him look at things from different angles in a way that just spinning the projection around didn't do. She could respect that. It was one of the few times the man was a proper professional. Now, if only he could be like that more often, she might actually like him. Hell might freeze over first, but that wasn't her problem.

She looked down as her hands auto-piloted their way to the row marker. The project was well on its way to being a sweater at some point. Much sooner than she had expected if they were going to spend many more hours drifting and tumbling slowly. Pretty soon she would have to break it off as she got to the bottom of the sleeve holes. But not for a while.

As she started on the next row around, she looked more closely at the projection. Djamila wasn't nearly as capable with the sensors as Aritza, but she understood enough to ask competent questions. And he had apparently appreciated trying to explain things to her, because he would get into the middle of a sentence and suddenly break off to go type furiously for several seconds before talking again.

The projection was starting to take shape. Different color stars appeared, strengthened, sharpened.

Apparently, minefields in space were like defensive fortifications on the ground. And she was an expert at those. Defense in depth. Overlapping fields of fire. Enfilade. Variety in range engagements. Lateral support. Stealth. Guile. Ambush.

It took patience to unravel, unlike the soon-to-be sweater in her hands. Watching Javier work reminded her of advanced tactical exercises she had run. Understand the terrain. Understand your enemy's plans for you and his tendencies. Find the weak spot he designed into the system as a honey trap to draw you in and kill you. Unravel the design until you found the hole he missed.

It had been four hours. She had watched Aritza like a hawk. Not because she expected him to actually commit suicide, he was too vibrant to just die so easily, but because she wanted to see him actually sweat. The man was far too lackadaisical.

Plus, he wanted to make sure they all went to jail, or the hangman.

Everyone else had forgotten that, but she occasionally still saw that look in his eyes. Usually when he was looking at her. That desire. That hunger. That hatred. It made her warm and tingly.

Besides, she smiled to herself as she worked, having a good enemy made you better. It made you keep upping your game, in a complex arms race to see who could win, especially two well-matched opponents.

So she studied him. Learned his traits and his tendencies. Watched him work so she knew his weaknesses, even as he worked to understand the long-dead designer of the trap they had entered.

You never knew when information like that would be useful.

From Javier's explanation, the minefield was a hive mind. There was no single controller they could kill to escape. Instead, a small part of the overall intelligence was in each little metal body floating around. It thought slowly, as a result. Patiently. Like a trapdoor spider. Waiting.

She understood that sort of patience.

Around them, dozens of killers floated. Big guns. Little guns. Armoured pods. Things to kill dreadnaughts. Things to kill shuttles. Every one of them powered by the solar wind and designed to last forever. It had been five and a half centuries, so far.

She had looked up the battle. *Pyrrhic* failed to cover the consequences.

Five fleets had all been functionally destroyed. But that was enough for *New London* to win the war and proclaim the *Union of Mankind* to a war-weary galaxy. The last significant challenger to their dream of a universal government had died on the planet below when someone had lost control of a terminally-damaged dreadnaught and it had plunged into the atmosphere, exploding only a few tens of thousands of meters above the ground, over the capital city of an entire Pocket Empire.

According to Aritza, the crater was apparently still visible from orbit, a bullet wound just rising into view below them in the near distance, beyond the minefield, inside the shell of death and destruction the war had left.

Afterward, there had been nobody to turn off the mines. Or the minefield had been laid by the victors as a way of salting the earth. Nobody knew the truth. It only mattered now because they were trapped in it, a small fly stuck in fresh sap, waiting for it to harden into amber. Or trapped in a web, waiting for the spider.

PART FIVE

Javier had finally found someone to dislike more than the amazon, Sykora. It had been a difficult thing. After all, the minefield designer had never given him a concussion, or worked him into utter exhaustion fixing bio-scrubbers, or any of the other things Sykora had done since they had first met, the first time she had shot him.

But the person who designed the defenses around *A'Nacia*? Here was a prime candidate for his considerable hatred.

Five hundred and fifty years had passed, more or less. The system this designer had built was still intact enough to threaten them. Javier had no doubt that the weapons were fully charged and just waiting to fire. He had sat here and watched the little battle-bots push themselves around with little pulses of energy, so he knew that most of them were working.

At least four different satellites were locked onto *Storm Gauntlet* with cannons of some sort at this moment. Certainly the weapons pointed this direction were things the hivemind that was controlling the field thought were hot enough to crush this ship if she turned out to be an enemy ship and not a rock floating around.

Javier wasn't sure the system wouldn't fire on rocks either. Eventually.

He would have programmed in that behavior.

He had, however, begun to solve the design of the system, sitting here and passively listening. Each satellite in the net broadcast an ID and a location on a regular basis, roughly every second, so the rest knew where each other was and what it was doing.

He had a catalog going. The forty-six closest ones, mapped and classified roughly into ship-killers, shuttle-killers, and scanners that just sat and watched. Some he had no clue what they did.

Their cryptography was weak, but still too strong for him to crack in anything less than a month, even with the navigation computer brute-forcing the signal.

And there were just too many of them out there for Mary-Elizabeth to take out in one salvo. He didn't trust that the shields would come up fast enough to help, or be strong enough to hold out. Someone had planned for dreadnaughts. That meant big guns.

Javier considered the ship's stealth cloak, but that just made it hard to scan them, not invisible. In fact, it had probably been what kept them alive, since they didn't scan like a starship to the stupid brain running things over there.

As soon as they did anything to change that conclusion, they would get boomed. And he was far too beautiful to die like this.

That's what he kept telling himself.

He looked down at his favorite tea mug and decided it had been empty long enough. And he was hungry. And *she* had been staring holes in the back of his head long enough.

Javier pushed a button to save all his notes and stood up.

"You're in charge," he said as he walked to the door.

"Where are you going?" she said, startled.

It felt good to throw her off balance every once in a while. She was just too damned smug, most of the time. Right now, she was furiously packing yarn and stabby things into a small cloth bag and trying to stand as he went past.

"Lunch," he replied, biting off the other replies that were rude, or snarky, or just obnoxious. Not today. He was too tired.

"Wait," she said, abruptly, "I'll come with you."

Javier actually stopped and looked back at her as the hatch slid open, holding his surprise in.

"You have the deck," he said, cruelly, as he stepped backwards and let it close on her surprised face.

***

JAVIER HAD GOTTEN food from the buffet line and an industrially-manufactured tea-substitute by the time she tracked him down in the main wardroom. Today it was something vaguely approximating previously-frozen burritos and what could charitably be called red rice, heavy on the vitamins and nutrients, light on taste.

He looked up as she walked up, just short of stomping.

"You aren't supposed to just walk off the bridge," she said firmly, professionally, scoldingly.

"What?" he smiled innocently, "you mean I should turn over operational control to another Centurion or qualified yeoman?

She wasn't standing close enough that he could actually hear her teeth grind, but the imaginary image in his head was close enough. He smiled up at her. Way up. Sitting, he was just about looking at her belt buckle.

She didn't respond, but instead slid the chair across from him back and practically threw herself into it.

"What have you learned?" she began the interrogation.

Javier carefully chewed the first bite of his burrito forty-two times, just like his mother had told him to do when he was a kid.

She was gnashing her teeth by thirty-four.

Javier swallowed, set the wrap down, and took a careful drink of the tea, slow to savor the industrial goodness that came of chemicals instead of dried plant leaves that he grew down in his botany hideout.

"Well?" she continued.

"The burritos aren't half bad," he said slowly, "but the tea just doesn't have it today. I would recommend the coffee."

"I meant about the minefield," she replied with a growl, exasperation filling her voice.

"It hasn't killed us yet," Javier said and stuffed another bite of meat-substitute-and-bean-thing into his mouth.

Chew. Chew. Chew.

"So you're no closer to solving the puzzle than before?" she sneered.

"Oh, I know lots of ways to solve it," he replied, eventually. "Most of them end up with us dead."

"Most?"

There was a really strange look in her eyes. One that might have been mistaken for hope, but that assumed that little miss invulnerable amazon giant had the least doubts in her ability to survive this particular situation. Especially when she had to count on Javier to save her.

Probably she just had gas.

"The rest are so completely insane that the Captain would never go for it."

"How do you know until you ask him?" she asked with a smile. Upbeat rationality from her was a new thing. Probably a trick, like telling him to look over his shoulder right before she slugged him in the jaw. Again.

"I'm trying to eat here, lady," he responded, somewhere between a surly growl and an exasperated sigh. It was where she left him, most days.

"You eat, Javier," she said with a smile. "I'll go get the Captain and you can explain it to him.

Javier? Really? Her?

He watched her start to slide her chair back, stop, and stare fixedly over his shoulder.

"Never mind," she said suddenly. "He's already here. You can explain it to him."

"Not falling for that trick," Javier said, stuffing another bite of burrito into his mouth.

"What?" She looked confused. Apparently hadn't had nearly enough caffeine today, or something. She sounded almost human.

He chewed, staring intently at her while he waited for a fist to appear.

"What do we know, mister?"

The Captain was suddenly beside him. Standing there. Really there. It was probably still a trick. Javier watched Sykora like a hawk. And chewed forty-two times. These people just did not understand good digestion.

A tap on the shoulder.

Crap.

Javier looked up, braced to be punched. Chewed. Made a face that boiled all the frustration of the last five hours into a single expression. Modern art. Sort of. Something. He was trying to eat here.

The Captain took a hint and sat down beside him. One of the evil Wardroom minions appeared with fresh coffee. *Why couldn't he get that kind of service?*

He ruminated on his burrito.

Oh, what the hell.

Javier smiled beatifically at the Captain. Go big or go home. Or maybe it should be *Go stupid or go home.* Because this was right up there with the dumbest things he had ever done. At least he was less likely to end up getting shot at or married. Again. Hopefully.

He took a sip of the tea-impersonator and set his mug down.

The whole room seemed to have gone quiet, like everyone was holding their breath waiting for his next words. Yup. Gonna get stupid. Might as well do it right.

"It's like this," he began. Swear to God that everyone leaned a little closer. It was almost like a scene out of a movie. Weird.

"The minefield isn't sure if we're a big rock or a stealthy starship," he continued, a little louder for the guy in the serving line who was leaning in. "As long as we sit here quiet, it probably won't shoot."

Javier looked around, faces were all turning slowly this way. He suppressed a giggle.

"However, if we do anything at all, we might set it off. Sensors. Shields. Engines. Even powering up the jump drive is likely to be enough."

"Understood. What are our options, Aritza?" Sokolov had that whole Captain Badass thing going today. It was impressive to watch.

"I thought about playing games with the gyros to see if we could drift out of range. We could, but it would take about three months if everything went right. Zero margin for error for that long. Unhappy option."

He sipped some more tea. The evil minions brought the Captain more coffee, and ignored him. He scored it a draw.

"Instead, I started looking at the mines themselves. Big,

dumb things. Couple of maneuvering pulse jets, banks of solar panels to keep the batteries at maximum charge. Some kind of gun. Either a multi-barrel pulsar, a big-bore cannon, or an Ion pulsar, depending. Enough to gut us like a fish, even with shields up."

"Encrypted?" the Captain asked. Good, solid *Concord* Navy veteran. If you can't kick the door in, pick the locks.

"Good enough. We might crack the code in 30-45 days, if we're lucky. Got a better idea."

"Oh?" The Captain had sense enough to look dubious. Javier's good ideas always tended to be *interesting*.

"Yup. Each mine rotates through a basic signal sequence. Eight and a repeat. Each beep, it also includes a simple x, y, z coordinate, zeroed on the old capital city on the planet's surface. I have no idea what each mine is saying, but it says them in the same pattern. We can use that."

"How?" the Captain looked somewhat askance at him. Smart guy. Waiting for the other shoe.

"We kill one of the nearby mines right after it sends a ping, and start broadcasting the same thing a second later. The hive mind controlling the field falls for it, ignores us, and we can use maneuvering pulses to back out of the field far enough to escape."

"You just said that powering up one of the pulsar turrets was likely to set things off," Sykora said, showing she was paying attention.

"Yup," Javier replied. "Someone will have to go over there with a limpet mine and blow the thing up manually."

"You?" she sneered audaciously.

"Oh, absolutely not," he smiled back. "Well beyond my capabilities. No, we need an expert in EVA and explosives. Somebody crazy. Somebody like the *Ballerina of Death*."

Yeah. That look right there. Smoldering hatred. If looks

could kill. Vitriol, distilled down to an aperitif and served with cheese and crackers. That look on her face almost made everything else worth it today.

Javier took another bite of his burrito.

PART SIX

DJAMILA HAD INSISTED Aritza accompany her here, at least as far as the landing bay. It was his brilliant idea that was going to save them, after all, wasn't it? Didn't he want to see it executed right?

The grumbles she got from him were reward enough. If he hadn't put her on the spot like that, she probably would have insisted she handle the task anyway. Nobody else on this ship was nearly as good at this sort of EVA work as she was. Period.

The bay looked strange. Aritza's scheme involved erecting a wall of spare metal plates across part of the bay, a meter back from the inner edge of the hatch.

"So that the scanners over there don't notice a sudden change in our shape and assume we're about to open fire," had been his explanation.

It sounded reasonable. At least as much as anything else coming out of his mouth ever did. As did cranking the door open manually so no power emanations leaked out and triggered a hostile response.

She completed a pre-flight checklist on her suit.

By the numbers. Careful numbers. She had had to leave her radio behind so she didn't accidentally signal anything to the killer mines that would be watching her as she separated from the ship. That would be a quick death.

Instead, one of her people was down here, familiar with the language of hand signals and in charge of her belayed line. There was no way in hell she was going to trust Aritza with that. But she wanted him with down here, uncomfortable, radio-less, forced to talk to himself while they waited to see if she lived or died out there.

He would have a front seat row. That little shit better appreciate it. Especially if he got her killed.

She leaned down to touch faceplates with her assistant. He was ready.

Javier next. He double-checked the electromagnetic box attached to her belt, gave her the thumbs up. She touched plates with him for any last minute instructions before total radio silence.

"Good luck, Sykora," he said simply.

He even looked serious. Awkward, but serious.

"You can't get rid of me that easily," she replied. It felt like a tease coming out of her mouth, even though she intended to make it a sneer. Too late to say something extra.

She saw his nod through the faceplates, followed by a frog-faced grin. So at least he was thinking the same thoughts she was.

Good enough.

She turned, and faced eternity.

A'Nacia was somewhere below the curve of the hull, off to her left.

In her immediate field of view, several bright points of light that represented killer satellite mines. Only one of them was close enough have definition. Javier's target.

It had taken several hours of fine manipulation of the

ship's gyroscopes, a tweak here, a surge there, but they had actually brought *Storm Gauntlet* to rest, relative to their target. Not close enough to make the system nervous, but enough that she had a fixed target from which to launch.

Her victim was just a little larger than one of the ship's landing shuttles, a little more than half a kilometer away. And she wasn't allowed to use maneuvering thrusters at all. It would be as pure a dive as she had taken since training, when they held emergency EVA drills and got scored on accuracy jumping across a gap half this size in nothing but a Skinsuit. While under fire.

Here she had her regular armored EVA suit, and a long hunk of line attached to an ankle in case she missed and they had to pull her back. And for when she succeeded and wanted to come home.

She fixed her target in her mind and pushed back against the plate inside the door. Others would probably have turned off the local gravplates and pushed off headfirst. That was a mistake. It went against everything they had trained for, and would throw off their aim.

She was going to take two steps and use the edge of the door as her final push-off point. Speed wasn't the issue here. Accuracy was. In raw space, you followed Newton, regardless of the rules that an interstellar starship violated along the way.

She looked around once, confirmed the rope, the assistant, the Science Officer.

Deep breath for extra oxygen.

Go.

First step. Second Step.

Darkness.

Free flight.

As pure as one could get outside of an atmosphere.

There.

Target acquired.

Coming in slowly, as planned. Others would have jumped too hard, and come onto their target so fast they bounced off before hand and foot magnets could grip.

Damn it.

She was going to miss a little high and a shade right. After setting a new *Neu Berne* record for accuracy at this sort of range.

It would be just far enough away that she would not land on it first shot.

Not having a radio was good. She could give voice to all the profanities she usually just howled in her head at such failures. Space didn't care. It couldn't listen.

Okay. Better idea.

She signaled her assistant to shorten his lead significantly.

She continued to fall. The nearest edge of the machine passed three meters to her left, just below her.

She braced as the line bit.

There.

Pendulum.

Djamila jack-knifed her upper and lower body together quickly, then relaxed. She reached the end of the rope and snapped down and left. She had missed, but only a little and not so much that they had to draw her all the way back in and send her out again.

The image of Javier as a fly-fisher nearly made her lose her concentration. It was a very good thing that in space, nobody could hear you giggle.

Instead, the line touched the side of the satellite and provided a fulcrum point. She swung slowly around the back of the mine, letting the line snug down and pull her in, like an ice-skater pulling her hands in as she twirled.

Contact.

Ferric hull. Generally smooth. Sensor bulbs there, there, and there. Maneuvering pulse thrusters on six points each, at both ends of a smooth cylinder some eight meters diameter and twenty meters long. Ship killer.

She looked around carefully. This was where they ran out of script. Had the designer anticipated this stunt and put a point-defense system in place to clear boarders? It suggested a level of paranoia and sadism well beyond anything else he had done so far, but who could ask someone dead for five hundred years?

Nothing moved. So far, so good.

Djamila detached the limpet mine from her waist and rested it against the hull of the satellite. Low-level magnets would hold it in place enough for her to work.

Stop. Look around quickly, and then slowly.

Nothing jumped out and shot her. Or bit her.

Good enough.

She armed the primary magnets and set the timer to ten seconds. It would be close, but not that close, unless her number was absolutely up.

Quick look around. Nothing sneaking up on her.

Flip the big red switch. Armed.

Push the button.

Run like hell.

This time, she just aimed in the direction of *Storm Gauntlet*. Distance counted way more than accuracy. She needed to be gone fast. If it worked, she was still attached to the ship. They could reel her in like a trout.

Again. Javier as a fly-fisher. She continued to giggle at the image.

Flash of light bright enough to cast her shadow on *Storm Gauntlet*'s hull.

In an atmosphere, something that big would have deafened her for days. And possibly pulped her with over-pressure shock waves.

Another advantage of space.

Storm Gauntlet's hull grew into a wall in front of her. She twisted and jack-knifed until legs were down and she was almost falling. Style counted here, at least with her people.

If you are going to demand excellence, prepare to give it.

She could still see the sign over the exit from the Senior Midshipman's Dorm at the *Neu Berne* Academy. Words to live by. And live well.

She landed like a cat, bounced slightly, put a hand down. But only one. Close enough to stick the landing and get full score from the judges, not that there were any, outside her head. Any that counted.

Djamila detached the safety line from her ankle and cast it back into space. They could reel it in much faster without her attached. She clomped her way along the outside, returning to the bay.

Mission very much accomplished, thank you.

Javier was there when she arrived.

She couldn't resist touching faceplates with him. "So, Mister Science Officer," she asked with a saucy tune, "was that adequate to your needs?"

He looked up at her far more seriously than she had expected. "That was the most amazing piece of free sailing I have ever seen."

Wait? Him? Impressed? Publically?

Crap.

PART SEVEN

Javier was just happy to be out of that damned suit. They had kept his when they killed his ship and took him prisoner, so it fit. That didn't mean he enjoyed it. Nope. Stale, industrial air. Metallic water. Claustrophobia.

Storm Gauntlet's air had gotten so much better since he had been put in charge of keeping the bio-scrubbers tuned, but it was still a pale shadow compared to what he had gotten to breathe on *Mielikki*. Even down in his botany station, it was only a faint reminder. The chickens helped.

Still, the amazon had been successful. If all went as planned, the Captain had flickered the ship's transponders at the right moment and they were now officially part of the minefield, beeping every second and updating everyone as they moved.

And they weren't dead.

Javier pulled on his leggings, tunic, and the extra jacket he had been wearing. It was still cold in the ship.

Of course Sykora was waiting for him when he emerged from his equipment locker. Probably tapping her foot theatrically too, though he hadn't paid that close of attention.

He trailed her to the bridge. This was the only view of her he liked, anyway.

"Well done, you two," the Captain announced as they arrived. The air was warmer here, so he had apparently felt safe enough to bring some of the systems on line. That would be good.

Javier was tired of wearing gloves while he worked. Shoes were already too much of a hassle. Hell, some days pants was asking too much.

Still, the Captain was giving them both credit. That would be good for some bribes from the crew. Markers against future need. You know. Stuff.

Javier moved to his station and powered it up fully. The big projection hung in the middle of the room, still.

It didn't look right.

He looked closer.

That was because they were moving deeper into the minefield, not backing gracefully out of range so they could escape.

"Captain," he said wearily. "Are we really going in there anyway?"

Sokolov smiled evilly at him. "You don't think I'd come this far and just walk away, do you? Get to work, Science Officer. There's a whole planet down there for you to survey."

Javier grumbled mostly under his breath as he brought systems live. They still couldn't send out any really good pings from the sensor suite, at least until they got safely inside the shell, but he could start the analysis.

These people were going to be the death of him.

He looked up and encompassed the whole bridge, especially that smiling amazon, in a disgusted frown.

Pirates and Philistines.

BOOK FOUR: PRISONER OF WAR

PART ONE

JAVIER'S TEA WAS COLD. Not that he was going to get up to get more. And the wardroom minions couldn't brew it right anyway. And if he drank any more, he'd have to go pee.

Plus, they were just about clear of the minefield, so now all the interesting parts would begin, knowing his luck. Because Heaven forbid these people do anything quiet and boring, ya know.

At least he could hammer the neighborhood with the occasional hard ping to see what was going on. The machines around him were dumb enough to think that was a targeting pulse. Sitting blind in the middle of a minefield had utterly sucked.

So, theoretically inhabitable planet below. Had been inhabited once, until a bright fall day in August Standard, five hundred and eighty-three years ago. Nobody had visited since. Or, if they had, nobody had escaped.

Boring looking planet. About half water and half land, randomly arranged by whatever the gods of chance and plate tectonics had found most pleasing recently.

Javier wondered about tsunamis down on the surface,

considering the vast amount of extremely large junk in orbit that was likely to fall eventually. Five fleets' worth of warships, plus every raider, scavenger, and pirate, save one, that had tried their luck over the centuries. Gravity was an unforgiving mistress and there was a lot of water to hit.

From here, the wound gouged in the face of the western hemisphere would rise in about thirty minutes. There had been a planetary capital there. Before. Ought to be able to pick up any radiation in a little bit, if there was anything significant. There weren't even lights down there on the dark side, so either the entire population had died, or just their technology.

Javier watched his screens as his data banks slowly filled with interesting tidbits.

He turned to the Captain as he considered taking the time to pee.

"What are we looking for here, anyway?" he asked, in his ten-year-old backseat-whining voice. He was good at that one.

Captain Sokolov barely glanced over as he watched the screen. "Money."

Okay. Yeah. The obvious answer. Translation: I have no clue what's here, we'll steal everything not nailed down, or anything that we can pry up.

Pirates and Philistines.

Still, it beat being dead. Or working as an agricultural slave on some forgotten, misbegotten backwater. At least the pirates had a sense of humor.

Centurion Djamila Sykora, Ship's Dragoon, walked in.

Most of them.

PART TWO

Zakhar had learned to watch what was going on in Aritza's head by the way his hands moved when he typed things on the console. Usually, it was a lazy, one-handed motion, two fingers and a thumb roaming the whole face to find keys and buttons.

When he got excited, or nervous, he used both hands, striking with precision and all ten fingers. *Concord* Fleet Academy training. When Sykora was around, back to one hand, slowly banging things out, like he was driving nails with his fingers.

If they both weren't so good, and, more importantly, so professional about it, he would have had to physically separate them a while ago. As it was, she was generally on his left and stayed away from the Science Officer on the right, with most of the width of the bridge between them.

Not that it would do him any good. Zakhar had seen how fast Djamila could move when she wanted to.

So Zakhar watched the Science Officer's whole outlook change, just in the set of his hands, when she walked in. He doubted that anybody on this ship, excepting possibly Aritza, would even recognize a reference to Pavlov, but he couldn't help himself. It was like a bell rang.

On the big projection, he watched the real time face of the planet slowly turn. They had already done something nobody had ever done. At least, that anybody had ever mentioned. If they could sneak in and out of here, he might have to bring back a bigger ship, maybe one of those monster cargo carriers, all hollow box, and see how much loot they could steal.

The old ships weren't going to be worth much as salvage after this long, but there would be logs, and sentimental value in things like personal effects and ship's crests, vintage fighters left alone on abandoned docks, etc. That would be worth something to collectors, especially since he had the market cornered.

Hell, Javier might make enough off his Centurion's share to buy his freedom, if it went really well. Maybe he could actually hire the man. He certainly wasn't about to just give back the trees, Javier would have to buy them. *Tell him that later.*

And then Javier's back flexed. Zakhar couldn't think of a better term to describe it. If he had been a cat, it would have been that moment when they arch their back and puff all the fur out.

It had that same feel to it.

He considered saying something, but he was afraid Aritza would realize that he was being watched so closely and clam up more. It wasn't as though he wasn't liked and respected. Javier was just a loose cannon on a pitching deck. A good Captain paid attention.

The profanity, only sort of quietly muttered over there, got attention from more people than just him. Several heads turned.

Javier repeated the word. Louder this time. He still hadn't looked up from his screens.

Zakhar watched Javier's head come up so that he was staring at the bulkhead beyond his station. Then it cocked to one side. Then it bent back down. Looking at the screen.

Javier repeated the word a third time, this one more of an incredulous whisper.

It was amazing how much of a conversation you could have, inflecting a single profanity different ways.

Javier turned, realized he had an entire audience.

"Captain," he said mildly, "you won't believe this…"

Zakhar agreed internally. Little that happened on this ship, especially when either of those two was involved, was believable to outsiders. And sometimes to crew.

He fixed Javier with his Command Eye. It made him feel like an evil wizard, eyeing his realm. And it usually worked, on the rest of the crew.

"Mister?" he replied, aloof, supernatural. *The Captain*.

"So *A'Nacia* has a single moon," the Science Officer began, pitching his voice into storytelling mode.

That was never a good sign with Aritza.

"I'm aware of that," Zakhar continued. Easier to just let Javier run.

"It's not as big as the homeworld's is, but it is still significant," Javier kept up his patter. "And because it is there, there are LaGrange points. Nice, happy little pockets in the gravity web where something will stay put after you leave it."

"Navigation 101, Aritza," Sykora called from across the way. She was apparently feeling feisty today.

"And as a rule," he continued, ignoring the *agent provocateur*, "I scan those as soon as possible, looking for things other people thought might be interesting enough to park there."

"Go on," Zakhar said. Javier had his own pace for this sort of thing.

"Most of the ships out here are just pieces or shells. Nothing that looks really valuable until we board some of them and take inventory. However, there is something interesting in the trailing LaGrange point."

"Define interesting," Zakhar's bad feeling had nothing to do with horror movie results. Javier was too much a sarcastic jokester.

Javier's smile probably would have chilled a lesser Captain to the core. He kept expecting the man to crack his knuckles ominously.

"Well, sir," Javier's smile grew, "there's a ship over there. It's an older model, but even the design is a century *later* than the battle that was fought here. After the minefield."

"So somebody else did the same thing we did and got here earlier. And?" Zakhar felt like the straight man here, but anything else would just slow it down. Nothing was dangerous or shooting at them, or Javier would have been acting more professional.

"It has power," Javier said simply.

"Oh."

There really wasn't much more to say at that point.

PART THREE

"ONE OF THESE DAYS," Javier ranted gloomily, "I'm going to learn to keep my big mouth shut."

"Ooh, can I sell tickets to that?" Sykora smiled down at him sweetly. "I'd be rich."

That woman had a knack. She just seemed to know instinctively where all his buttons were, and how far she could push them without making him do something about it.

He decided to talk to her boobs instead of her face. Craning his head back got old, anyway.

"For you, maybe never," he said. "What would we do if you retired?"

"You'd do something stupid and get yourself dead inside a week," she added a layer of sugar on top.

"Children," Captain Sokolov said. Quiet. Firm. Commanding.

Javier refused to listen to that part of his lizard-brain that had been trained to salute even when he was dead asleep or falling down drunk. Bad precedent. The man might come to expect it. Then where would they be?

They were, right the moment, back down in the loading bay, waiting for the engineering crew to finish extending the boarding tunnel, mate it, and override the airlock on the other side so they could board. It felt like they were getting ready for a picnic. Kind of looked like it, too.

Captain Sokolov was there to see them off. Sykora had a smaller-than-normal group of her killers, armed for invading small planets. Javier's occasional assistant and sometimes minder from engineering, Machinist's Mate Ilan Yu, was present.

Sykora's two pathfinders for planetary work were also there: Sasha: the short brunette with the nice hips, and Hajna: the skinny blond with the long legs. Nice girls. Cut-throat card sharps.

Javier took inventory. Since they were expecting power, heat, and hopefully air over there, at least after some repairs, everyone was only wearing skinsuits today instead of the big armoured suits like Sykora had used to kill the mine.

To various loops and belts Javier had attached bits and pieces he had rifled from his planet-side gear. The little bag with low tech stuff like a magnetic compass (currently useless), matches (no scrub to burn), paper and pencil (good for mapping), a small metal knife (it didn't vibrate, or have a laser edge, or collapsed monomolecular edge, or anything cool), and his handy little hiking trinket that combined a very cheap magnetic compass, a thermometer, and the symbols you should make in the dirt in an emergency.

The only thing high-tech he was taking was Suvi.

Externally, she looked like a small gray grapefruit, covered with knobs and things. Externally, she was just his short-range autonomous sensor remote, with an extra surprise. When the pirates had taken his ship, *Mielikki*, he had managed to smuggle out the AI who ran it, and pour her into the remote. And kept her his little secret ever since.

Since then, he had upgraded her electronics about as far as he could without people asking suspicious questions. She didn't have her original memory core, but all of her personality could fit now and she had pretty much all of her log files and enough books to keep her busy for a few years at least.

He looked around to make sure he had space and then tossed her into the air as he pulled out the matching portable computer. It would take her about thirty seconds to re-baseline the bay in visual, ultrasound, radar, and infrared, with a stack of dials and gauges giving him various readings on people and equipment.

There had been enough time to upload what he knew about the ship over there, plus some of the mission parameters, so she was at least as prepared as the rest of them. And probably smarter.

The engineering crew coming out of the boarding tube brought him out of his fugue with a jolt.

"We have a seal over there, sir," the woman said, addressing herself to him instead of the Captain standing next to him or the Dragoon beyond that. When had he gotten put in charge?

Still, this was a technical task, and they were nerdy people. He at least spoke in a language they could follow, some of the time. Unlike little miss amazon killer here.

"That's good," he replied, absolutely at a loss for her name. "Status over there?"

"Didn't get too deep into their diagnostic system, but we're pretty close to level," she said. "Gravplates are dialed down to about one quarter, so be careful or you'll bonk your head. Air reports breathable and acceptable pressure, but stay prepared anyway. Temperature is only a few degrees above freezing water, so you'll want to dial your suits up now."

Javier glanced around. The people surrounding him were

almost scary competent. Paying attention. No questions. No complaints. Already setting switches and dials, based on the word of an engineer they barely knew.

He put actions to thought and turned his temperature up to a balmy twenty-five degrees. A beach would be nice about now.

Javier checked all the gauges and dials on the remote's control board, watched them adjust themselves for the environment over there and smiled to himself as he started typing.

Good morning. Ready to go? JA

Affirmative. Can we steal it so I have someplace nicer to live?

He suppressed a snort. If the pirates around him found out about Suvi, his life wouldn't be worth warm spit. That was why she was hidden in the remote. They forgot about the device most of the time, and he could work on it without arousing suspicion.

Let's wait for these chickens to actually hatch?

<pout />

Yup, it was going to be one of those days.

He looked up to see Sykora watching him from across the way. She would be in charge as soon as they stepped onto the other ship. As well she should be. You never knew when you were going to find monsters out there.

Just because mankind had been exploring the galaxy for more than four millennia and not found anybody didn't mean there was nobody to find. Just that we hadn't gotten out far enough, or soon enough, or something. And not all monsters were aliens.

"Ready, mister?" she asked.

He looked at the heavily armed people in the party. "Can I have a sidearm, just in case we run into monsters?" he asked. It was mostly pro forma at this point.

"Aritza," she smiled calmly down at him, "I'm the bogeyman."

53

PART FOUR

Suvi watched the hatch grind slowly open, at least slowly to her, and directed her sensors into the other ship.

275 degrees Kelvin, so warm enough to keep water liquid and not rupture things. Atmospheric pressure at the low end, roughly two thousand meters equivalent elevation. Gravplates set to one quarter standard. Not as light as Homeworld's famous moon, Luna, but she would have to hop across the gap in freefall and dial everything down so she didn't mash into the ceiling.

Piece of cake.

She watched Sykora, the big woman Dragoon, *the dragon lady*, nod to Javier. He pushed a button on his little console that normally handled the flight controls. Now, it just displayed a happy face in her cockpit and started up mood music for flying.

Today, she was flying an early heavier-than-air aircraft known once upon a time as a helicopter. Hers wasn't as loud as those primitive machines, although she had considered adding sound effects for verisimilitude.

Like the two pathfinder women, Suvi went in first.

It was a boring place. Industrial design heavy on gray, with square corners that actually looked welded instead of cast. *How droll.*

The hallway from the airlock was relatively short. The dimensions were human, 2.5 meters wide and tall. Coarse texture on the deck plating for traction under gravity. Boring walls.

The whole ship appeared to exist on a single deck, laid out long and narrow, pointy at one end and flared at the other, from the pictures Javier had uploaded.

Suvi flitted to the place where this little hall emptied out onto the longer hall that ran down the central axis of the ship. In her mind, she echoed Javier's question. *Why couldn't we just bring it aboard the pirate ship to open it up?*

She replayed Captain Sokolov's comment: "Because I want it go boom outside the ship's armoured hull." He reminded her of her first Captain, Ayumu Ulfsson, back before the probe-cutter *Mielikki* even had a name, back when she was just a hull number scouting for *Concord* fleets during the Great War. Maybe it was the Academy training. It hadn't stuck with Javier, but it had with Zakhar Sokolov. It brought back some of her earliest memories.

Suvi smiled.

From the long hallway, she could see more than two thirds of the ship. She added dimensions and schematics to the information she was displaying on Javier's screen. To the right, the hatchway that probably led onto the bridge. At the rear, a huge, armoured bank-vault of a hatch. Obviously engineering. You wanted things going boom back there to stay back there.

Someone had painted a really strange logo onto the wall a little forward of the crossway. At first, Suvi had dismissed it as art, but from here, it looked official, and kinda important.

For fun, she locked her targeting brackets on the image

and beeped Javier's console extra loud. Through the tiny fish-eye lens he had installed on the control portable, she could see several people jump suddenly.

Suvi giggled.

She missed having access to *Mielikki's* data banks. That thing looked like a symbol, but it was outside her current knowledge base. She would have to rely on the much-dumber computers running *Storm Gauntlet* to hopefully have an answer. *Mielikki* would have known instantly.

She missed being a starship.

A few moments passed. She watched the group consult. Guns came out. Javier apparently was arguing with them, but there was too much noise for the little microphone to wash it all out. And she didn't want to listen to an argument today.

Javier surprised everyone by walking away from the group and entering the boarding tube. She could hear him clomp up the walkway towards her, followed a few seconds later by the big woman, Sykora, and the rest. The profanities bouncing around in the cool air seemed interesting. She filed them away for future use. You never knew when they might be useful.

Suvi watched Javier enter the ship through one of her cameras. She put his picture on his screen to say hello while the rest of her attention scanned the hallway.

She could hear little radio emissions bouncing around the ether. Javier had never bothered to load cryptographic software onto the remote, so she couldn't listen in to whatever conversation the strange ship was having with itself. It didn't sound particularly exciting, from the strength and frequency of the transmissions.

And Storm Gauntlet *was WAY too stupid to be able to do something like that all by itself.*

How could humans get around the galaxy in a ship that didn't think? I mean, sure, they had before good AI's had come along. But still, she was way smarter and way faster, and rarely fat-fingered a control. Whatever.

Javier stopped beside her, looked her in the eye with a smile, and cracked open the faceplate to his skinsuit. He took a shallow sniff, cold air being detrimental to organic lungs, and nodded.

According to her readout, the air should smell acceptable. Boring, without all those complicated trace signatures that plants, and soil, and chickens gave off, but not lethal and not particularly uncomfortable. To someone accustomed to *Storm Gauntlet*, probably a breath of fresh air, literally.

Humans were weird. But, hey, it paid the bills.

"Aritza," the big woman boomed, across the air and the radio, "what the hell do you think you are doing? This ship could be dangerous."

"Nope," Suvi heard him reply with a chippy glibness. "Not with that."

He pointed at the logo as he spoke.

It was a blue circle, reasonably thick, with a green ellipse painted across that. Overall, exactly fifty-two centimeters tall and fifty wide.

It had been painted by a human, rather than an AI. AI's were too fussy for that level of wobbliness.

Okay, most AI's. I might have done it in a lighter green, and added some sparkles to the paint. And maybe a few stars for effect. You know, ART.

From her knowledge of human eyesight, it might appear to be a planet with rings. Weird looking rings, but rings. There were a lot of weird-looking things out there. She had been a galactic surveyor for years. She could testify.

"What is that?" Sykora asked over the clamor as the rest of the boarding crew caught up.

"Something the *Neu Berne* military programs probably

didn't cover," Javier said quietly, forcing her to lean down to listen.

She hated that, according to Javier. Suvi got the impression Sykora might be grinding her teeth right now. Certainly, she took a breath before she answered.

"Oh?"

"I only know it because I spent a weekend at a religious retreat a while back with the modern incarnation of those people," Javier said evasively. "Weird folks. Generally harmless, but weird."

"Pot, kettle," the short, brunette pathfinder injected into the conversation as she arrived. Sascha was an extremely smart woman, from what Suvi had been able to surreptitiously observe.

Javier made a face at her.

"I got over it," he snapped sarcastically. "Anyway, that is the emblem of a group of pacifists from a very long time ago."

"Pacifists?" Sykora asked, dripping sarcastic honey on her words.

Suvi loved to listen to the tone and inflections the woman used. It was so different from Javier's, or anyone she had known in the *Concord*. One of these days, she needed to convince Javier to take her to *Neu Berne*.

Sykora did something with her hands. Suvi watched Sascha and Hajna, the other pathfinder Javier played cards with, take up station looking fore and aft, guns drawn. The others stayed back in the side hallway, prepared to run or fight.

As far as Suvi could tell, Sykora was the most dangerous thing on the ship right now.

Javier watched, bemused.

"Pacifists," he repeated. "Shepherds of the Word."

"Which word, Javier?" Hajna asked, kneeling beside Javier and covering the aft hallway to engineering.

"Aritza," Captain Sokolov's voice came suddenly over the radio. "What are you talking about?"

Suvi got a head start and transmitted the image of the logo back to the ship. They would think he had done it. He would back her up, later.

A moment of silence passed, breaths baited.

Suvi imagined the Captain asking his ship's computer for more information. She envisioned an ancient butler, shambling along looking through a musty library for an ancient book. She giggled.

"Javier," the Captain continued, "are you sure?"

"Sure enough," Javier responded. "Plus, it's been a very long time, so it's not like there's anybody here to bother us."

"Agreed," the Captain replied. "Sykora, stand down for now. Those people really were pacifists. Pay attention for surprises, but you should be safe from booby-traps."

PART FIVE

Javier refrained from smugness. Outside. Inside? Different story. After all, Dad loved him best. See?

That thing on the wall had brought back a lot of memories. Most of them things he'd rather not remember, these days. He'd kinda forgotten how ugly things had gotten in his life after his first ex-wife left and his career with the *Concord* Navy started to ramp down with the budget cuts.

Out of work. Out of married. Down on his luck and himself. Amazing he had survived. Even gave religion a try at one point. For a long weekend. Those people had just been too weird to be believed.

He was much better now. Even Sykora really only occasionally got him mad enough to go back there. Okay, weekly. But that was down from daily. Hourly. Whatever.

The Shepherds of the Word. The Prophet of the People. The *Union of Man*. Things from the history books.

That painting there meant that this ship had, at one time, belonged to one of the actual Shepherds, one of the close followers of Rama Treadwell himself. The Prophet who had preached a universal brotherhood of man that should be reflected in a union of worlds. *The Union of Worlds.*

The battle that had destroyed *A'Nacia* had been, in its own bizarre way, the culmination of Treadwell's life and teachings, twisted though the outcome had been. Even after he simply disappeared from history while traveling in deep space, his words had resonated. Some people had thought that that disappearance was what triggered the Unification War.

Javier wasn't sure. He was kind of sketchy on that history anyway. After all, it was just about 650 years ago. And the Battle of *A'Nacia* was nearly 600 years ago, at the other end of the Unification War.

The Shepherds had faded, down the centuries, until there were only a few small monasteries tucked in out of the way places that were too damned cold and frowned on gambling and drinking. Silly people didn't understand what made human organizations successful.

For luck, Javier touched the painting. He spun in place and scanned the hallway, correlating naval architecture with what he had learned in school.

Skinsuits didn't allow it, or he would have cracked his knuckles.

"Right," he said, mostly to Sykora. She and Ilan Yu were the only two looking at him, anyway. "Bridge at that end. Two cabins right behind it on one side, office and stores on the other. Wardroom and Rec room behind the hallway, most likely. Big engineering section back there."

"Recommendations?" Sykora asked. There was no doubt she was in charge here. None. Devil take the hindmost if you asked her.

"We have power," Javier replied. "Heat would be nice, and I want to see if the environmental system is up to handling a dozen people." He smiled extra evil at Ilan. "You'll get to practice on a very old system."

"Joy," Ilan replied with a tired sarcasm. Still, it was his job, and he was pretty good at it over on *Storm Gauntlet*. This should be a much less complicated system to fix up.

"Very good," Sykora decided. "Drone first, then pathfinders, then me. Civilians behind that and one guarding the rear."

Javier shrugged, pretty sure he and Ilan were the civilians. Still, let the gun bunnies absorb any incoming fire. Better that way. He pushed a button and let Suvi take point. She would protect him better than Sykora. She'd already proven that.

So he ambled along. Sykora's skinsuit just emphasized how nice her butt was. He could follow her around, pretending to pay attention to the remote, while Suvi was actually doing all the work. Too bad the rest of the Dragoon was so much less fun.

The words on the door didn't really catch his attention. It was just another one of the side doors headed back to engineering. There were a lot of them. Turned out the ship was a little longer than he had expected. Or had smaller rooms.

After a beat, his brain clicked. *Cryonics Lab.*

"Oh, crap," he whispered, forgetting that he was arm's length from a keyed-up, heavily-armed lunatic.

She spun in place and drew her pistol in one motion, even before he could say anything to stop her.

Next thing he knew, she had it pointed between him and Ilan, safety off, prepared to unleash complete mayhem. Or what she probably called Tuesday.

"What?" she whispered hard at him. There was nobody to shoot. She sounded disappointed.

Rather than speak, Javier stuck out one hand and

touched the little brass plate next to the door. He tapped it twice for emphasis.

"You don't suppose…" He let the rest of the sentence trail off into the surf of its own accord.

"How old did you say this ship was?" she asked, standing a little more erect and holstering the weapon. She was no longer eye level with him.

He looked up and shrugged. "The design dates back about five centuries or so. I'd have to look at the deck plate on the bridge for her actual keel date."

He thought about it for a few seconds. "Really freaking long ago."

She looked at him hard. Javier nearly jumped in surprise when she shrugged back at him. "Anyone in there isn't going anywhere, anytime soon. Let's get engineering ship-shape."

Hopefully, she wasn't relaxing around him. He'd have to do something stupid, or personal, or both, if that happened. Little miss amazon ramrod never relaxed. He would bet money she slept at attention, although he had no intention of ever finding out.

"Move it, people," she called out.

Suvi was already hovering at the hatch to engineering.

Javier knew she was just waiting, as she could have triggered the mechanism herself. But a remote wasn't supposed to be that smart, so she played along.

Javier just pretended as though anything he pushed on the console actually did something. He made a mental note to ask her what actually happened, next time they were alone. It was probably something pretty silly, knowing her.

Sascha had to open the big armoured hatch to engineering instead. Hajna and Sykora covered her with weapons out. He and Ilan just stood around. The guy at the rear walked backwards with a cannon pointed up the hall.

Some people.

Like all good, military-grade starships, engineering was separated from the rest of the hull by a fairly solid internal airlock. Fires didn't breath deep space, and if something went wrong back there, sometimes that was the only solution. Sucked to be an engineer at that moment, but they kept emergency breathers in every drawer for a reason.

Suvi passed through the airlock first. Javier typed away on the keyboard as she provided a running commentary.

Not as big as I was expecting.

Older design. Significant technological leaps during the Great War. It's what made you possible, young lady.

Still, it looks rough. Unpolished.

He had to agree. What she showed inside there had an almost amateur look. Maybe civilian was the word. Almost every starship he had been on in three decades was either active-duty military or retired surplus. There were certain rules of architecture that every navy followed. Physics were physics.

This looked like something thrown together from parts someone had salvaged from a junk yard. While drunk.

Of course, if they had been as serious about the whole vow of poverty thing in those days as now, they might not have had the funds to build custom ships to spec.

Not that poverty had been the breaking point with him, that weekend he had spent at the monastery. No, it had been that stupid requisite vow of chastity. And sobriety.

Javier could see the jumpdrive. Big, honking monster sitting there in front of twin pulse thrusters. That thing over there was probably an auxiliary power reactor, just from the color. Air scrubbers all along that wall. Way smaller than he expected, so either more efficient design than he thought, or smaller crew.

"Looks good," he said finally. "Everything accounted for.

Environment safe. Only wandering monsters are out in the hallway."

That got him a sour look from all three girls. Of course, he wasn't holding a gun on a closed hatch. In a ship that was centuries old, stuck inside a minefield. Did they think they needed the whole van Helsing routine?

"Sascha and me next," Sykora commanded. "Hajna with Aritza and Yu last."

"Aye, sir," replied the girls and the gun bunny, on cue.

Javier nodded sloppily. Her, he might salute, just to piss her off. He might even do it right, just to show her, exactly once, that he could.

He refrained. Barely.

He typed instead. *Company coming. Stay sharp.*

Si, commandante.

See? That, right there, was how you did snark. He was so proud of his girl.

Javier thought about going back up to the Cryonics facility while the amazon was elsewhere, but decided that the gun bunny would just interfere and stop him before he could do anything interesting.

Might as well wait.

He was quickly bored, waiting the three minutes for the two women to cycle through the airlock.

Anything you want me to do while we wait?

Not that wouldn't give you away. Look for rat droppings. That will be the clue that the environmental systems are compromised.

Fresh or dried?

After this long, anything you can see is a problem.

It would, however, give Sykora something to shoot. That would probably improve her humor. Silver linings.

It seemed like forever before he and Ilan finally made it onto the big deck. It was noticeably warmer back here. Not warm, but the various machines seemed to be turning over regularly to provide power from the solar batteries. And the life support systems had been left on. That was a good sign.

Or a bad one. Hard to tell. Still, Javier had three armed women handy. Not exactly a harem, but this wasn't exactly his idea of a bordello. Generally.

"Ilan," he said, shaking himself from his reverie and dragging the machinist's mate along with him, "this is the environmental system. I'm familiar with the theoretical design. You get to learn it. Don't do anything stupid. Yet."

"Gosh, sir," Yu replied with an equal-parts sloppy and sarcastic salute, "I shall endeavor to live up to the standards of excellence you embody."

Javier did a double-take, just to make sure the man was kidding. You never knew with engineers. He might have gone all professional and stuff. Bad juju.

Javier gave him the stink-eye, just in case, and then headed in the direction of the APU. It seemed to be putting out a baseline.

What, however, needed a baseline? Life support would barely require a quarter of the juice flowing out. The other options made him nervous. More nervous. Almost as nervous as his paranoid cohorts.

Okay, maybe not that bad, but bad.

Mentally, he made a list as he cracked open an access panel and shined a pocket light in. *Storm Gauntlet's* Chief Engineer, Andreea Dalca, could probably have it tuned and humming in half an hour. She was that good. One of her people would probably take a half-day, just to be sure. They might need to string a power-line over from the big ship, if what was using the juice was what he feared. Not a good thing to interrupt.

Engines were next. Primary tanks were long since drained, but could be filled up pretty quickly by cracking hydrogen from the water tanks that showed mostly full. In a pinch, Javier had once hijacked a comet and used a small pulsar to cut a section out to melt for the water.

If all else failed, there was a whole planet below. Water would not be a problem. Whether the fusion torch would work, that was a different question. And not his concern. Let Dalca's people solve it. Tomorrow.

"Javier, I thought you said this would be hard," Ilan mock-whined from the corner.

"Nope," he replied with a smile. "Sledge-hammer stupid. Brute force machine."

"I know," Ilan smiled. "Wash the screens, flush the primary coolant and recycle it. I don't have all the tools I need, but this won't take more than an hour. Why do we use bio-scrubbers?"

"A quarter the size, Ilan," Javier noted, "and about a thousand times more efficient. This air would get pretty stale after a month."

Javier looked around at the jump engines and the thrusters. "Ship like this is designed to sail point to point in small jumps, and land on a planet every two to three weeks, or dock with a station. Not to make long sails like *Storm Gauntlet* does. And it would still have a very small crew doing it."

"Well," the machinist's mate said smugly, "I can fix this easy enough."

"Good," Javier said. "Make a list of what you think you need and then go do the same thing on the APU. I expect we'll need to bring over a portable generator or run lines across the way so we can bring it off-line and work on it. Don't worry about the engines until the Chief comes over and inspects them."

"Roger that, sir."

Javier turned and realized that all three women were

staring at him. Not hostile. More like open-mouthed shock. It was a weird feeling, surprising this particular group. Felt good.

He forgot, sometimes, that they never saw him in his engineering and fix-it mode. *Concord* Fleet officers were trained for this sort of thing as a matter of course. Hell, fixing the bio-scrubbers on *Storm Gauntlet* when he first arrived was the original reason he hadn't ended up as a slave on a farming world.

He smiled innocently at Sykora. "Nobody to shoot here," he needled. "Orders?"

PART SIX

Javier stood outside the hatch and took a deep breath. Ilan and the male gun bunny had been left in engineering to clean things up. He had the three women with him, four with Suvi, as he contemplated the little brass plaque hung at eyeball level.

Cryonics Lab.

To Sykora and Hajna and Sascha, just words. They weren't trained in this sort of thing. Hell, almost nobody was, these days. The technology was used so much less today than it used to be. Mostly for medical purposes, in a total catastrophe. Ships didn't need it, as life support systems were so much better now and Jumpdrives could hop so much farther in one go.

He took a second deep breath.

"Why are you nervous, Aritza?" the amazon asked, her voice almost blowing warm air in his ear.

He did not, quite, jump out of his skin. He did turn and look her in the eye, from a distance of about eight centimeters. Biting her seemed rude. Kissing her, more so.

Both would be equal amounts of surprise as payback. Maybe tomorrow.

"What's on the other side of this door," he said, just loud enough for the three to hear him.

Safeties clicked off in the ominous silence.

"Oh, put them away," he half-snarled. "There's nothing in there to worry you. You're the bogeyman, remember?"

That nearly got him punched. By more than just Sykora.

They did holster the weapons, though, so Javier could relax.

Suvi took up watch above and behind, where she could see down the long hallway and over any of the bodies in the way. She was prepared, in case she needed to rescue him. Again.

Javier turned back to the door and placed his palm flat on the access plate. Given the circumstances, he could see someone actually locking it, but that would be an oversight, not a design feature.

The hatch clicked back a centimeter into the room and slid out of the way on powerful pneumatic sledges.

Javier reached out a hand and caught Sykora before she could complete her step forward.

"Not yet," he whispered, almost intimately as she rounded on him. "Let it breathe."

"Breathe?" she asked, almost as quiet.

"It has been closed up for a very long time. The air is likely to be a little foul with volatile trace elements."

"What's in there, Javier?" she asked, turning her head to scan the room beyond.

Javier? We're back to Javier, are we?

"Not what," he said, a little louder, for the other two to hear as well. "Who."

"Who?" That got her head spun all the way back around

to face him. A hand was on the pommel of the pistol, ready to draw and fire.

Javier leaned forward and sniffed carefully at the breeze blowing softly into his face. A little rank. Extremely dry. Cold, where the rest of the ship had been merely cool. Right about what he had expected, from the things he had read, once upon a time.

Some days, he hated being right.

Javier walked forward instead of answering, one hand still on Sykora's arm, but more as a guide than a restraint. As if he could actually stop a woman like that if she set her mind to something.

She trailed along anyway, half a step behind him, probably prepared to throw him into the dragon's maw to give her the half-second she would need to draw and kill it. It was how she thought.

The room was larger than he had expected. Or rather, the walls were where they should be, but less space was taken up.

Based on the size of the ship, he had expected two, or possibly three big boxes in here. Sarcophagi. Coffins.

There was only one, tucked back into the corner, although he could see the power couplings for two more coming out of the walls.

One was enough.

Javier walked to it quietly, hearing the slight hum of the device in the still air, feeling it in his feet when he got close and stood over it.

Ancient kings on the Homeworld had been buried like this. Big black box, three meters or so long, two wide, one tall. This was metal instead of stone, and the inscriptions on the sides were medical instead of propaganda.

The goal was still immortality.

He glanced over at the three women to make sure they were still with him. They were, but their faces showed growing apprehension. They were beginning to understand things, at least a little.

He heard Suvi shift a little forward just inside the door, where she had a good view of the room and could still interfere if someone tried to sneak up on them. They had cleared the ship room by room, but Sykora was a stickler for those sorts of details and he wasn't in the mood to argue with her. Not right now.

Javier leaned forward for a better view. The top half of the sarcophagus lid was clear, covered over with a thin rime of frost. It was active. Whether it had worked was a different story.

He reached down pulled off a glove. He would need the body heat.

That warm hand wiped away the layer of frost ice from the glass.

Inside, the face of a young woman, instead of a desiccated mummy. She was dressed in a simple black shirt, with the same logo worked on both sides of the collar.

Javier blew out a breath he had forgotten he was holding.

"That's who," he said, quietly, reverently. Without a nav computer, he couldn't even begin to guess the odds of success. Machines like this were supposed to be used for much shorter periods. Months. Maybe as much as a year, in a pinch. But centuries? The mind boggled.

"Who is she?"

Javier wasn't sure who spoke. It was a quiet whisper, almost an intrusion into the realm.

"She is a Shepherd of the Word," Javier said simply.

ZAKHAR LOOKED DOWN at the coffin. This was why they paid him the big money, so he could be in charge at moments like this. Life and death decisions. Command.

His Science Officer stood to one side, consulting quietly with the Chief Engineer. Andreea Dalca was a broad, compact woman, a product of high-gravity world. She was a first rate engineer, and a complete introvert. How she and Javier got along so well was a mystery for the ages. But it worked.

Right now, they were deep in a very esoteric, technical conversation. He followed about a third of it. Nobody else in the room probably got a tenth.

Sykora and her two pet pathfinders were here as well, staying mostly out of the way in a corner. The room wasn't crowded, and he wasn't sure they would leave if ordered, given the situation. It was certainly unique for him. Best let it slide for now.

Out in the hall, he could hear others moving around. Mostly Dalca's people, doing the sorts of maintenance tasks any ship accumulated, even at rest. Given the age and state of the ship, they were already money ahead if they could get it to any port. If they could locate the right sort of collector or museum, they might be rich.

That would bring a new set of problems. He would burn that bridge when he got there. They had a much more interesting problem today.

What to do with the ship's owner?

Andreea and Javier seemed to think that there was a good chance she could be revived with no long-term damage. At which point, she became his problem.

Zakhar hadn't set out to be a slavemaster. He was a *Concord* Fleet veteran, retired, damn it. They had saved the galaxy when *Neu Berne* had set out to conquer it. That it had been done before his birth didn't reduce the fact that they were supposed to be the good guys.

Javier looking at him that way didn't help. It was a reminder that they were brothers, of a sort. Men who took the oath.

Unconsciously, he found himself playing with his class ring. *Concord* Fleet Academy, Class of '49. An Officer and Gentleman, by Act of Congress Enshrined.

If he thawed her out, he would have a brand new kitten. What was the ancient saying? If you saved a life, you were responsible for that life. He could order the plug pulled instead, but he didn't want to know which of his crew would actually obey that sort of order. Or how much of his crew he would lose, on a personal level, if he became that sort of Captain.

There really was no doubt what his answer would be. Javier and Sykora had to have known that. But they had been in complete agreement that he had to come over and make it. This was only the third time they had ever done something like that.

So here he stood.

Zakhar tried to remember what little he knew about the founding of the *Union of Man*, and the ancient Prophet, Rama Treadwell. Not much. *Union of Man* history had never been his thing, growing up. Too busy with racing speeders and sports teams.

He knew even less about the religious order known as Shepherds of the Word. Something about a group of wandering mystics looking for their lost Prophet in the depths of space, and carrying the Word like missionaries to all the worlds of the *Union*.

Javier had said that the Order still existed in a few places in the *Concord*, or the quieter corners of the worlds that had once belonged to the *Union of Man*. Before the Great War. Probably a museum somewhere on *New London*, if he cared enough to look. Maybe someday.

He leaned forward again to look down at this woman. She looked young. Sleeping peacefully, like the princess in the ancient fairie tale, or the strange little man who walked down into the fairie mound and lost centuries when the morning came.

Zakhar estimated her age to be in her mid-twenties, barely out of her childhood, although he had been commanding an armed pinnace at that age. Officer and Gentleman.

What to do with this kitten, after he found her by the side of the road and took her home?

Command.

"Javier," he said firmly, projecting his voice clear into the hallway. It was a skill that made Captains. "How long to thaw her out?"

He noted how serious the man had become. Nothing like the normal class clown. That usually meant bad things. Today, it just meant serious. Like he was thinking the same things.

Javier had once been in command. He knew.

"Given the lack of a Ship's Surgeon," Javier replied, "I would recommend wiring the box to a portable generator and moving her close to *Storm Gauntlet's* medbay first."

He paused there and looked down at the coffin. Zakhar could see the wheels spinning in his head, calculating options and timelines. Were all Concord Fleet officers like that? Probably. Came with the territory. The Good Guys.

"After that," the Science Officer continued, "I think we bring her out just about as slowly as the box will let us. Not like we're rushed for time here."

"You volunteering?" Zakhar asked gruffly.

The man shrugged eloquently. "You got anybody else?"

"No, mister, I do not," Zakhar said. Command voice. Command decision. "You will take charge of the rescue."

He turned to his Engineer. "Andreea, you are in charge of getting the ship ready to fly if possible. It's too big to transport out inside *Storm Gauntlet*, and too valuable to section up unless we have to. Questions?"

She never once made eye contact. She never did. Sometimes, he felt like he should keep his shoes extra polished, just because she would be looking at them instead of his face.

"No, Captain," she said quietly. "I estimate we will have a complete status in eighteen to twenty hours."

"Good enough," he replied. "Javier's kitten first, Andreea."

He turned and started to leave the room. Sykora fell into step with him, to his right and half a stride back. Just like always.

"Kitten?" she whispered as they walked. "What are you planning to do with her?"

"I'll know that, Djamila, when he succeeds."

"Aye, sir."

PART EIGHT

Javier felt like the greater of two evils. Any two evils.

The Purser's people had emptied out a nearby storage room for him, giving Kianoush Buday, his tea mug artist, a chance to see the whole affair unfold as he had several crewmembers sled the big sarcophagus over and then connect it to ship's power.

It dominated the empty room, laying there like this was a state funeral.

He was the Science Officer, so he was in charge, right? Said so right there on the side of his mug. This was Science. Javier can handle it.

He looked at the hatch, as if it was transparent. Medbay was just across the hall, door locked open and machines on standby, in case something went wrong. He hadn't bothered to tell them that if something went wrong during the thaw, she would be better off never waking up from whatever dreams had filled her long night. They wouldn't understand until it was too late.

As far as he knew, nobody had ever been successfully kept

alive this long under cryo. Not because the theory was flawed, but because there was no reason.

You found the survivors or you didn't. She had had to be a prisoner of war, in a war that had ended five hundred and eighty-three years ago, to even be a candidate.

Javier sipped his tea and ruminated. How could you explain to someone the rise and fall of the *Union of Man*, the Great War with *Neu Berne*, or the rise of the *Concord*? Depending on how long she had been here, would she even know about the latter two?

What do you do when you wake up, Rip Van Winkled out of five centuries of history? Everyone you knew wasn't even a footnote any more.

And then, to top it all off, you've been captured by pirates.

Javier was a well-treated and well-respected member of this crew. But he never forgot that he was here paying off a debt as a slave. Honor. Duty. But still a ransom.

If he brought her out of the fugue, wouldn't she be just another slave? And did she have any skills that could make her valuable? Or would she be so hopelessly out of date that all she had to fall back on was a strong back on a mining colony?

Javier looked down at the sleeping face and realized that she might find a fate worse than being an agricultural slave. It was still, to some extent, a man's universe.

The hatch opened before he could sink too deep into a funk. A body slipped in, closed it quickly. The lock keying into place got his attention.

Sykora.

He fixed her with a questioning stare. She had no business on this deck right now. None.

She was impervious to his look as she strode into the room and stood across the box from him. She stared back.

The quiet hung.

Usually, the air crackled with negative energy when he was around her. Today, nothing. Just silence.

She spoke first.

"Have you decided yet?" she said quietly. It was a tone he had never heard from her before. Calm. Serene. Inquisitive.

"Decided what?" Javier wasn't going to play whatever game she was up to. Not right now. He would just keep score. There was always tomorrow.

"If she lives or dies," the tall woman replied. She had a hard look on her face.

"I don't make that decision, Sykora," he said. "Sokolov does."

"No," she refuted him simply, "he decides what happens after that. You decide if she ever wakes up."

Javier's eyebrows threatened to crawl backwards over the top of his head. He tended to forget that underneath that tough killer exterior was a first-rate mind. Until she did things like this to remind him.

He would have been happier not being reminded.

"You look down and see a woman," she continued, "and wonder if she can find a place in this world, or if she would be better off not having to make that choice."

Javier shrugged, unsure where she was going but unwilling to gainsay her.

"You were raised to think of women as weak," Sykora said. "The *Union of Man* was the worst, but the *Concord* is not much better. In *Neu Berne* or *Balustrade*, women are the equal of men, in all things."

"And?"

She leaned forward, almost conspiratorially. "If that was a man, would it be a question?"

He leaned in as well. "Would a man be at as much risk of finding worse things in life than being a slave in a mine?"

She looked down, considered the peaceful face between them. "Is it a fate worse than death, Javier? I've seen men and women indentured to brothels. As slaves go, they tend to be better kept than those in mines, or farms. It is a business, after all. She might be happier if that happened to her."

"Oh, I know," Javier replied finally. "There are a number of places the Captain might sell her. Me? I'd head to one of the big worlds and ask for a finder's fee from one of the big universities to cover the expenses. They would love to have someone who lived that long ago, just to talk about what the world was like."

"And what makes you think the Captain won't do that?" she asked him, harsh vitriol creeping back into her voice.

"Because I'm a slave, Sykora," he said flatly, harshly. "Dress it up all you want in fancy language, but I owe a bonded debt to that man. One of these days, maybe, MAYBE, I will be in a position to pay it off and get my own life back."

"And are you treated poorly, Mr. Science Officer?" She leaned closer, getting right down into his face.

He leaned closer as well. "You killed my ship, cut her into parts so that I'll never get her back," he snarled hotly. "You drag me all over the damned galaxy doing pirate shit, so that I'll hang with you if we ever get caught by someone big enough to do the job. And I am not a free man, Sykora. You could walk away from this ship if you wanted. Just walk out the hatch at the next station we visit and never come back." He tapped his finger on the top of the box as he spoke. "I do not have that luxury."

"You were a mouthy punk who pushed as hard as you could, when I met you," she snarled back, nose almost touching his, voices so low that someone at the doorway might have mistaken them for lovers. "You were offered the choice to be here or somewhere else, somewhere where you could have escaped if you wanted. You chose to stay. You do not get to complain now."

The room was suddenly tiny.

"So I should just trust that you people will do the right thing?" he growled back. "That Captain Sokolov really is a good guy and it will all turn out? Based on what?"

She stopped and drew a breath.

It broke the spell.

She leaned back, flushed. She blinked.

"Because it is not your decision to make," she said quietly, tapping on the sarcophagus. "It's hers. Anything else makes you just as bad as Sokolov."

If she had just slapped him, a good open-palmed right hand to the face, he probably would have been less surprised.

Javier bit back any retort that might have come out of his mouth. He leaned back as well, drew a breath deep into his chest, tried to burn off the surge of adrenaline that threatened to overtake him.

They stared at each other for several moments, neither moving.

Javier nodded, mostly to himself, partly to her.

He reached down and flipped open a panel by his right knee. Inside, a big red button. Obvious in its intent and purpose, scribed in half a dozen written languages, just in case.

He leaned into it, watched it start flashing slowly. Off. On. Off.

He straightened up and looked at the tall woman standing across the sarcophagus from him.

"Who are you?" he said querulously.

She straightened out to her own great height, towering a whole head above him in the tiny space.

"I am a woman who will not take any shit in a man's world, mister."

Javier nodded. That was about right.

PART NINE

It had been nine hours. Javier was keeping himself awake with heavily caffeinated tea and regular potty breaks. He had napped some, early on, with Sykora, of all people, keeping watch while he did, lights dimmed and all sound off.

This day had gotten completely and utterly weird.

Now, there was nothing to do but wait.

The sarcophagus had a timer function, but he had cranked the system down to the lowest setting to bring the woman out of her sleep. He figured that would do the least amount of damage, and let her recover best.

If the theory of this machine was the same, she was slowly being refilled with the same synthetic blood that had been keeping her alive for so long, with the anti-freeze elements slowly being weaned out. The longer she had to recover, the better. At least in theory.

Any Ship's Surgeon, even the drunkard that Sokolov had apparently fired three years ago, would have made him feel better right now.

Javier wished he had Suvi handy to talk to, but that would raise too many questions from the crew as well. And he really wasn't prepared to deal with Sykora again any time soon, not if her latest gambit to drive him crazy was going to look like this.

He sipped his tea and thought dark thoughts.

The hollow thump caused him to blink. He didn't think he had been asleep. Hell, with this much tea in him, he wasn't sure when he would next sleep.

Thump. Right. Activity. Progress.

The sarcophagus suddenly started to hiss, just like a tea kettle reaching the boiling point.

Javier was out of his chair and across the room in almost one bound.

The machine had broken the internal seal.

He could smell the gases it was releasing. It smelled like a pickled artichoke he had eaten once, at a parish fair.

The room picked up the faintest hint of fog, even as the air circulation system kicked itself into overdrive and sucked the strange vapors down and away from him, probably to vent into space.

Below him, the glass slowly retracted into the belly of the system, like a vehicle window rolling down, with the faintest puff of dust.

Javier held his breath, mostly out of anticipation. He vibrated, but that was the adrenaline mixing badly with the caffeine. He rocked back and forth on his feet, like a kid waiting for his turn to open birthday presents.

Javier stopped when he caught himself.

I am a professional. I am this ship's Science Officer. I need to act like a grown-up. At least for a little while.

He looked down at the girl asleep with bemusement.

Up until now, she had been a problem to solve. First, transporting her intact from the other ship over here, and then getting the power switched over. Finally, defrosting her like a ham.

He hadn't taken the time to actually look at her.

Her hair had been tucked up under a knit hat to keep it away from sensors and probes, but a few stray hairs peeked out. Redhead. With a splash of cute freckles across her nose and cheeks.

A very feminine face, soft across prominent cheek bones and a soft jaw. Skin that his mother would have called porcelain.

He couldn't see much more of her, other than the black shirt with her Order's logo on both sides of her throat. A Shepherd of the Word. An honest-to-goodness missionary.

She wouldn't have been old enough to know the Rama Treadwell himself, the ship wasn't that old. But she would have remembered the *Union of Man* in the early days, before entropy and bureaucracy set it. Before the dream had soured.

Not that he would tell her. Let her find that out on her own. Wasn't that what Sykora had said? She deserved the chance to make her own decisions, rather than having them made for her, however well-meaning those decisions might be.

Eyelids fluttered.

Breath restarted with a gasp, drawing cold air hard down into her lungs.

Pretty blue eyes opened. They didn't focus, but he didn't expect them to.

He leaned back as the lid of the sarcophagus cracked along the edge and slowly began to pivot up and away. It was a well-designed system he had no intention of interfering with.

Inside, she was wearing a full bodysuit, made from some stretchy black material and covered with a mesh of sensors and tubes that had kept her safe and alive. A little more solid than he liked his women, but in relatively good shape for a woman who had just set the galactic record for a nap.

"Can you hear me?" he said in a quiet voice. Everything from now on was going to be intuition and luck.

He was rewarded with a couple of blinks.

"You are safe now," he continued in his best bedside soothing voice. "Let me know when I start making sense."

She turned in his direction and came back from a thousand kilometers away slowly.

Her whole vocabulary seemed to consist of blinks and alternating deep and shallow breaths.

Javier had had days like that.

"Good morning, sleeping beauty," he said, unable to help himself.

She croaked at him, so there was sound as well. She made a face, too, trying to find the words, or the concepts of the words.

"What can I get you?" he asked, leaning a little closer. That seemed to help, as her eyes began to focus on his face.

"Water," she whispered back at him in a bone-dry voice.

Well, crap. That I can't do without leaving you alone in here. Shouldn't do that.

Javier looked down at his mug of slightly warm tea.

Oh, what the hell. She's human.

He handed her his prize tea mug carefully.

"This is tea, young lady," Javier said, carefully enunciating and hoping he was making sense. "It's still a little warm, but also kinda chewy. Hope you like it green."

He helped her wrap both hands around the metal cup and then let her tip it backwards slowly, sipping some of his prized green tea in small dribs.

After a few sips, she lowered it and fixed him with those bright blue eyes.

"How the hell did you get here?"

Javier smiled. This was going to take way longer than just one pot of tea.

PART TEN

ZAKHAR SAT and watched Javier take his first sip of tea, after working his way slowly through the act of making it. It had seemed like meditation in motion, watching him move, almost like a robot.

The man looked exhausted.

The rest of the room sat dutifully quiet as well, although Zakhar was sure they were bubbling over with questions.

Javier finally sat his mug down.

Interestingly, the first person he made eye contact with was Djamila. Something subtle passed there. Something deep and intense.

She nodded back to him.

Whatever it was, it must be good. Zakhar wondered if he would ever get that story.

"Four hundred and eighty-eight years," Javier said tiredly, answering one of the first questions, and by extension, several others.

He took another drink.

"Her name is Wilhelmina Teague," he continued, "and

she was born on *New London* in the early days of the *Union Of Man.*"

Zakhar let the room hang for a few seconds, but Javier was apparently done for now.

"What does she know?" Zakhar said quietly. The rest of the room appeared to be in some level of shock. It was one thing to envision that stretch of time, but it was something else entirely to have it there on the table in front of you.

He watched Javier shrug. Again, the eye contact with Sykora. Another message passed.

"She knows how long she was in there," he said. "She knows that the minefield is still intact, but doesn't know how we survived it. I don't plan on telling her."

He took another drink of his tea. Zakhar waited patiently.

"Right now, she's asleep in medbay, being monitored by the robot. She didn't want to sleep. We talked for nearly three hours, but she's got no reserves to draw on. That will slowly change over a month or so."

Zakhar nodded. About what he had expected.

Javier was taking all this way too seriously. It was possible that the man was planning to steal the ship and try to escape with it. Unlikely, but he had to consider the option.

"Andreea," he turned to the Chief Engineer, "what's the status of the ship?"

She never looked up from her little portable computer as she spoke. She never would. "We will have to transit the minefield to get far enough away to test the Jumpdrives, but they appear to be in good order. I'm sure the calibration is off by an order of magnitude or more, but we can fix that after one test jump. The ship was rebuilt to run with only one crew member, but I wouldn't trust it without at least an engineer, a machinist's mate, and a navigator aboard. It is in remarkably sound condition, all things considered."

Zakhar smiled. He knew a collector who would probably outbid everyone for such a ship, more so for one with such a history. And would keep quiet about the provenance of such a prize, at least until they could come back and do a more thorough job of looting the system.

He would be rich. They all would be wealthy.

His eyes fell onto his Science Officer. Javier might even make enough to buy his contract out on his share. Not the trees, but some things were negotiable. He did, after all, owe the man his life and his ship. They would have been dead ten seconds after the jump without him. And dead again in the minefield without his patience.

He would miss the man. Not that he would ever admit it. Javier had made *Storm Gauntlet* a better place.

Zakhar turned to his Navigator. "Piet, what are the Astrogation computers like?"

The big Dutchman smiled grimly. "Five hundred years out of date, Captain," he said quietly. He did everything quietly. "I have taken the liberty of downloading the data to storage and replacing it with as much data from our own systems as I felt prudent. There is additional space for whatever course you wish to plot from here."

"Good job, everyone," Zakhar let his warm smile embrace them all. It almost felt like the old *Concord* Fleet days with this crew, especially when they were humming along like they were now. Although Javier and Djamila NOT bickering was a point of concern. Still, those were indeed problems he could trade up for.

"I know this has been much harder than we normally encounter, but it will all be worth it."

He took a sip from his own half-forgotten mug of coffee.

"Javier," he said, "when she is awake again, I would like to meet her."

Again, the look exchanged with Sykora. What the hell were those two up to?

"First thing on my list, Captain," the Science Officer replied, "right after breakfast. I had the medbot give her something extra to sleep, so she will be awake in about eight hours, famished."

This time, Sykora nodded first. Something was going on and he had a feeling that it was a secret those two would take to their graves.

"Until breakfast then," Zakhar said in his command voice. Would he ever get that story?

PART ELEVEN

JAVIER ESCORTED Wilhelmina with one arm, like a proper gentleman and everything. He was pretty sure she was up to the walk, but best not to take chances. Not today.

She was dressed in an outfit Kianoush had picked out for her, from things carefully stored over in the little ship.

Black pants baggier than was the style these days. A tight, long-sleeve shirt, also in black, with a gray sleeveless tunic over it tabard-style and a black leather belt. The same logo from both sides of her collar was emblazoned on her right breast, about the size of a goodly grapefruit, embroidered into the cloth.

The hair, once released from confinement and cleaned in a long, hot shower, had turned into a strawberry blond braid down to her shoulder blades in back, with cute little bangs in front.

Standing in her stocking feet, Wilhelmina had turned out to be a few fingers taller than Javier. Not in Sykora's range, but probably the third tallest woman on the ship. He would have to line them up to be sure.

Javier felt like the hero escorting the magical Princess to

meet the King. There was something to that. Not that he would ever say that out loud to Captain Sokolov. Man might get fancy ideas, and then where would they be?

The Officer's Wardroom had laid out for a special affair this morning. It almost looked like a State Dinner, with fine china and silverware Javier hadn't even known the ship still had, left over from the Fleet days.

Off to one side, Captain Sokolov and Sykora sat at a small table, obviously cleared and organized for such an affair. Javier led Wilhelmina to a chair across from the Captain, and seated her like they had trained him in the Academy days. It was amazing how quickly all those classes in deportment were coming back to him.

He was going to have to do something stupid and crass. Not now. But, later. Now was too important.

Javier slid into the seat across from Sykora and smiled at her. She nodded back with a smile. This was going to be even weirder if she was going to be nice to him and everything. It might be time for a few good practical jokes on the woman, just to keep things light and stupid. Friendly Sykora was too much like Trapdoor Spider Sykora.

But right now, Wilhelmina. Her time. Her luck. Her fate.

Javier did a triple take when he realized that someone had brewed tea and steeped it already. His awesome mug was in place and steaming vaguely.

He tried to say something suave about his tea, but it came out more like a Tamarin, babbling and pointing ineffectively.

"Pixies," the Captain smiled his evil smile.

That did NOT help the matters in Javier's head.

The two women silently looked at each other, and then the two men. Javier felt an eyeroll coming on. Fortunately,

Wilhelmina didn't look anything like his second ex-wife, or that would have been just too much weirdness for one day.

"Ms. Teague," Captain Sokolov began instead, "I am Zakhar Sokolov, Captain of the *Storm Gauntlet*. Welcome aboard. You've met my Science Officer. This is my Dragoon, Djamila Sykora."

She shook hands with both across the table. Her manners were up to the test today. Javier kept his running commentary inside and smiled. The tea was even done right. *Wonders.*

"Thank you for rescuing me, Captain Sokolov," Wilhelmina purred. "What would be the fastest and safest way for me to get back to *New London*?"

Oh, did I forget to mention she was a genius-grade intellect?

Javier smiled, remembering what it felt like to talk to her, even newly awakened. Him playing jacks. Her playing the ancient oriental game of *Go*. Her draining him of information until she finally had to sleep, and let him recover. She didn't look like an intellectual vampire.

They never did.

Javier watched the Captain make a moue as he considered his response.

At no point had the word *pirate* come up in the previous conversation, but she was a very, very sharp woman.

"I realize," she continued blithely, "that I represent an unexpected complication in your salvage operation, but I am prepared to work for my passage."

This time, the Captain's eyes darted to his Science Officer. Javier took a sip of a really good cup of tea to hide his smile.

Any response was defeated by the arrival of breakfast, served by the wardroom stewards.

Javier had a moment of panic as he considered that the pixies and their evil minions might be planning to poison him, but they would have done that already with the tea. So, this should be attacked like a proper final supper before the execution. Word to deed.

"Where did you get fresh eggs?" Wilhelmina said with wonder.

"I raise chickens," Javier replied around a piece of marmaladed toast.

She put her fork down and turned to stare at him. "You RAISE chickens?"

"When you feel up to it, I'll take you down to the arboretum and introduce you to them."

That got him a look. Pirates didn't have arboretums. Most pirates. They certainly didn't keep chickens. Not in any of the stories she would have known.

Javier smiled. That would be an even longer story.

"Why *New London*?" Sykora asked as they got back to the task of eating. "Why not someplace like *Bryce*, the capitol of the *Concord*?"

"I considered that, Dragoon Sykora," Wilhelmina replied.

"Please, call me Djamila."

"Djamila. Thank you. Please, call me Wilhelmina."

She took a sip of coffee to organize her thoughts.

"I was born on *New London*, five hundred and eighteen years ago, if the clocks are to be believed. I began my journey there, seeking to follow the footsteps and mission of Rama Treadwell. I would like to see my hometown, just once, before setting out on my mission again."

"Mission?" Sykora asked.

Wilhelmina smiled. "Did they ever discover what happened to Rama Treadwell?"

"No, they never have," Sokolov replied quietly.

"Just so. I am a Shepherd of the Word, Djamila. I might be the last of my kind, at least until I can train others."

"But the Unification succeeded," Sykora said, confused.

"No," Wilhelmina replied firmly. "*New London* conquered a goodly chunk of the inhabited galaxy and proclaimed a *Union of Man*. That lasted until someone else decided they should conquer the universe and enforce their own definitions of good and evil on everyone. Rama Treadwell's dream was a place where all people were free to define and encompass their own destiny. Not just the wealthy, or the lucky. Every man. Every woman. Every person. From what Javier has told me, the *Concord* is trying, but even more in need of the words of the Prophet than ever."

Both Sokolov and Sykora turned to look at him. He stared back, challenging them to say anything. Prudence got the best of them.

"We're trying, Ms. Teague," the Captain murmured.

"We're all trying, Captain," she replied with empathy. "It is a hard road. But one that must be traveled. We must bring the light to even the darkest corners and darkest hearts. That is what Rama Treadwell taught."

And that, was most certainly that.

Minutes passed in companionable silence as they ate.

The Wardroom stewards cleared the plates and brought fresh coffee. Wonder of wonders, a small pot of steeped tea, even done right. Obviously, pixies.

Javier wondered when the ambush was coming.

"So, Ms. Teague," the Captain broke the silence, "If you are set on traveling to *New London*, that represents another complication. We aren't likely to be in that sector any time soon. The closest we are likely to get in the next six to nine months is *Meehu*. Once in the near future for supplies before we return here to *A'Nacia*, and then again after a second trip."

"I can work for my passage, Captain, both here and after

I make it to *Meehu*" she said quietly. "It won't be the first time. Ships are always looking for good crew. I have several degrees, including accounting. And, after a time to return to proper form, a strong back. I can learn most things quickly."

She took a sip of her coffee and glanced sidelong at Javier. He fought a losing battle to keep the grin off of his face.

"One other thought," she trailed off.

"Yes?" Captain Sokolov took the bait.

"Javier tells me that you don't currently have a Ship's Chaplain."

He smiled. The looks on both of their faces was worth every bit of what was going to be coming to him for this.

PART TWELVE

ZAKHAR TRIED to hide his surprise.

Djamila stomping into his office was a new experience. She was the most professional soldier he had ever known. Yet here she was, practically gnashing her teeth, assaulting the floor plates with her boots.

Starting with breakfast, today was just turning out to be all sorts of special. Zakhar could only imagine what fun Javier would bring, at this rate.

Before she even stopped moving to salute, he pointed at the chair. "Sit."

As she did, Zakhar experienced some level of juvenile payback, watching her realize that the chair had already been adjusted to her height. The look on her face was priceless.

Normally, the first thing she did when her butt hit a chair was manipulate it for her so-much-longer legs. She was the tallest person on the ship. Nothing fit.

Unless you knew she was coming.

Zakhar refrained from smiling at her. Command face.

He let her stew for a few moments, composing herself from being knocked off kilter.

"I have a problem," he opened the bidding strong. Jacks or better.

Her eyes got that cagey look that told him far more than just responding would have done. She really was up to something. And Javier was involved. Helping, perhaps.

Perfectly crazy.

He waited, but she had closed down and was happy to call. At least this round.

"I have found a lost kitten by the side of the road," he continued, watching her like an owl might observe said kitten.

"Yes. Kitten," she replied, all clammed up.

Apparently, this was not how she had expected the conversation to start out. Probably wouldn't be the conversation she expected to have. Tough.

"Normally," he continued, drawling out the syllables, "I would happily add such a kitten to the list of trade goods for sale at the next station or land-fall."

The way she flinched said far more than words. The chair actually creaked with the stress of her suddenly gripping it with one hand.

He dangled that last part for an extra moment.

She wouldn't take the bait.

"I have the impression, from more than one crew member on this vessel, that people would prefer that I make an exception to the normal rules, at least in this case."

She nodded slowly, warily.

It dawned on Zakhar that his Mistress of Close Combat had learned some useful things about political maneuvering over the last few years. Probably from watching him. The Djamila who had joined his crew, once upon a time, would not have been able to hold her tongue right now. She would have been ranting at him, as was her style, in the privacy of his office, never a word whispered about it later.

This new woman had gone quiet, reserved, poised.

What the hell was going on?

"So," he continued, "should we get out of the business entirely?"

He left it hanging.

"There are times," she whispered, finally breaking her silence, "when it is appropriate to bend the rules."

WHAT?

For a moment, Zakhar was nearly convinced that he had a doppelganger sitting in his office.

This woman embodied a life following the hardest rules and order. It provided her context, and, often, solace.

He took a sip of coffee to prevent the absolute shock spreading across his face at her words.

"For her," he finally said, after he could swallow his shock and his coffee.

"For her," Djamila replied, barely above a whisper.

What the hell was going on?

"What about others?" he said warily. "Javier Aritza, for example."

The open palm slamming onto the top of his desk was loud enough to make him nearly jump clear out of his chair. Zakhar made a mental note to check the surface for a dent, later.

He would have broken his hand, hitting something that hard. She probably hadn't noticed.

"That little punk had it coming," she hissed savagely. "Still does."

Okay, then. That settled that question. For a moment, Zakhar had been afraid that the two of them had patched things up and secretly started dating. Crazier shit had happened in the last seventy-two hours.

"So the rule is generally sound," he nodded, drawing the words out, "but not in this instance?"

She nodded back, dropping back into her quiet place, breath still a little ragged. He watched her fight her heart rate back to normal.

Between Javier getting serious and Djamila getting flexible, Zakhar wasn't sure the vessel wasn't completely overrun by Aritza's pixies. It made about as much sense. Perhaps more.

"Why?" he said flatly.

He was still the Captain. This was his deck, his vessel. But it only worked with a good crew. And something had changed.

It was like an infection, brought aboard by the Shepherd, without her ever saying a word.

And he would have never believed it, had he not been there.

Djamila took a deep breath, held it, released.

He wondered, briefly, if she would even tell him. Something was going on with her and Javier. And two less likely co-conspirators he had a hard time imagining.

The pause stretched. He could see the thoughts and words racing around in her eyes.

"Djamila," he said quietly. "It's not enough, even for you. I need to know why."

He heard her breath catch. The room had gotten that quiet.

"Opportunity," she whispered back, so quiet that he might have not heard it, had he not seen her lips move.

He fixed her with a quizzical stare, unwilling to speak and break whatever spell had taken this warrior woman and suddenly made her…something. Not vulnerable. She didn't do vulnerable. Human, perhaps? Had he ever seen her *merely* human?

"I'm here because you gave me a chance, when *Neu Berne*

was done with me," she continued, still barely audible. "Andreea had run out of chances with the *Balustrade* Navy. For others, it was the same way. Aritza is working off his debt-bond, but even then, he has had an opportunity that he wouldn't have had, if we, if you, had sold him to some colony as slave labor."

"And Wilhelmina Teague?" he asked into that vast gap that had suddenly opened between them.

Djamila paused, composing her thoughts. For moment, her guard was down.

The look in her eyes was almost pain. From a woman who prided herself on being tougher, harder, meaner than anyone else. Always.

"When she's little," she said in a tiny voice, "her daddy takes her on his knee and tells her stories about princesses and dragons. And she grows up with those fairie tales. Sometimes she remembers them, and wonders what her life could have turned out like if it hadn't gone down the particular path it did. How it might have been different."

Zakhar sat quietly, marveling at a side of Djamila Sykora he had never *imagined* existed. He sat perfectly still, unwilling to break the spell that had come over her.

"And Wilhelmina is a magical princess, sleeping for centuries and then awakened."

The image of Javier Aritza as the dashing hero waking the princess with a kiss almost made him laugh out loud. Being the Captain was enough to hold it in.

What the hell was going on?

"We," she said quietly, "you, have the opportunity to do something from a fairie tale. You can rescue the princess like the fairy godmother, or put her back to work scrubbing floors, like the evil stepmother."

Zakhar had been called many things in his life. Officer and Gentleman. Captain. Warrior. Pirate. Other things less savory, sometimes only in the voices he heard when he tried to sleep.

He had never been an evil stepmother.

For a moment, the silence just hung. He seriously considered actually hiring that woman as Ship's Chaplain, if for no other reason than to see what *Storm Gauntlet* might turn into. He had already seen sides to Aritza and Sykora he never dreamed he would.

What other surprises might the future bring?

Zakhar realized that Djamila was hanging on pins and needles, watching him.

Again, not vulnerable, but human. Perhaps vulnerable. Especially if she suddenly saw him as a fantasy king and Javier as a heroic prince rescuing damsels.

He nodded to her.

She breathed out and deflated a little.

"Thank you," he said quietly, solemnly.

She nodded and rose. After a moment, the spit-and-polish Sykora made her appearance, ramrod straight and perfectly poised. She snapped off a salute, pivoted, and exited the room, once again every inch a recruiting poster Dragoon of a pirate ship.

Nobody would ever believe him, even if he had someone he could tell this story to.

Zakhar keyed the comm built into his desk. "Kibwe Bousaid," he said, activating the system to locate his aide, wherever he was on the ship and beep the nearest comm.

"Bousaid here," the voice came back after a beat. Rich, warm. A man with a background in radio. How had he ended up on *Storm Gauntlet?* What was his story? Zakhar realized that he had never asked.

He never did. They were pirates. Some things were better left unknown, and the rest were frequently far more mundane than esoteric.

"Sokolov. Please locate Ms. Wilhelmina Teague and ask her to join me in my office."

"Will do, Cap'n."

Zakhar leaned forward and rested his chin on his hands.

How had any of them gotten here?

Some time passed before a knock at the hatch. He opened it, expecting his aide and Teague.

Javier stood there.

"Two minutes?" the man asked hopefully.

Zakhar nodded and watched the next round of craziness ooze into his day.

Javier sat without asking, as was normal with the man.

The look of surprise on his face was almost as good as it had been on Sykora's.

"So she's already been here," the Science Officer said as he adjusted the chair.

Zakhar nodded. This round was going to be two of a kind or better to open, and Javier was a better player than Djamila. Let him start the bidding.

"Did she get an answer she liked?"

Zakhar had to pause and deconstruct that question. It made no sense. Unless the two of them were up to something.

The two of them.

Together.

What the hell was going on?

Zakhar cocked his head sideways and looked at the man before him.

"Why?" he asked, every inch the Captain right now. He felt the deck threatening to slide out from under him.

"I have two speeches prepared," Javier grinned back at him. "Didn't want to waste your time rehashing things if you had already made that decision."

Whatever it was, Zakhar was suddenly unsure if he

should keep Teague around forever, or get rid of her immediately.

The ship had changed. He wasn't sure it was a good thing.

"She's a most amazingly interesting woman, when you actually get to know her," Javier said, apropos of nothing.

Zakhar paused, considered, studied.

"Teague or Sykora?"

Javier gave him a frog-faced grin that made his eyes almost disappear.

"You spend time talking to someone like her," the Science Officer continued, "and learn things. Sure about her, but also things about yourself you have forgotten over time. They come back and you remember them again from when things were good."

"I see," Zakhar said, unwilling to commit to more just yet. He didn't, but it was a useful placeholder until he did.

"I remember a quote," Javier said, again wandering off on another tangent that made no sense. "*We do things not because they are easy, but because they are hard.*"

"And what would be the hard choice here, mister?" Zakhar growled quietly, two old Bryce Academy school chums having lunch.

If only.

Javier grinned.

"It's not that hard, really," Javier replied. "Teague already knows her ship is salvage, and she's okay with that. You send her to *Meehu* with the ship when it goes, and she makes her own way from there. She'll be fine."

"And what's the hard choice?"

Javier paused and swallowed. His eyes got very cold.

It was a look Zakhar was familiar with, from his own mirror. A man making hard choices.

"When you sell her ship, the crew will get their shares,

the officers theirs. And I'm betting you'll find a very happy buyer, since we just did the impossible and found a working ship five centuries old, with a fantastically awesome story. Am I close?"

"Close enough, mister," Zakhar said.

Javier studied his face for a moment.

"I would like Wilhelmina to get my share."

Zakhar's stomach felt like it had been punched. He would have bet that Aritza couldn't have topped Sykora today in surprising him.

And lost.

Moments passed. Two men staring at each other across a desk.

"Why?"

"Something she said made me remember who I always wanted to be when I grew up."

"Teague or Sykora?"

But Javier just smiled at him.

IMPASSE

A KNOCK AT THE HATCH.

Zakhar had a chime, but it was rarely used. People preferred the tap. More personal, perhaps.

He pushed the button to open the hatch.

Aritza stood in the door with a clipboard in one hand and a mug in the other. He entered and plopped down in the chair without invitation.

Zakhar looked up at him silently, waiting.

"The other ship is away with Wilhelmina and Sykora aboard," he said. "Just made their first out-system jump en route to *Meehu*. Should take Piet about eight days to arrive there. Are they really going to hire a big freighter to come back out here?"

"They are," Zakhar nodded. "We'll use the same trick to get the freighter inside the minefield as we did to get the other two ships through."

Sykora was likely to get good at the technique of killing mines by hand. If he didn't get her killed. Or she decided to kill both he and Aritza for making her do it.

"Why not hire a minesweeper?" Javier asked.

"I don't want to share my toys, mister," Zakhar growled across the desk. "After I've taken everything I want out of here, then maybe we'll talk about hiring a minesweeper. Right now, like you said, it's a haunted ships' graveyard."

He watched Javier shrug and take a drink before setting the mug down on his desk. It was an old battered porcelain mug from a bakery on Merankorr.

"Where's your fancy mug, Aritza?" Zakhar asked. Come to think of it, he hadn't seen the man without it in some time.

Javier looked down at the mug for a moment, and then looked up at him with a smile.

"I sent it with Wilhelmina," he said, "as a memento of her time here. Wanted her to remember all this in a good way."

"I see." Zakhar craned forward to look into the mug. "Is that coffee?"

"Yup," he said, taking a sip. "Trying new things."

Javier stopped and looked extra serious for a moment.

"I also wanted to thank you for sending Wilhelmina off with enough money to do something good with her life."

"It might have been enough to buy out your contract, you know," Zakhar said quietly.

He watched the man shrug eloquently.

"It wouldn't have been enough to ransom my chickens and my trees."

Zakhar smiled a tight, tiny smile. "Figured that out, did you?"

Javier rose with his own smile and made his way to the door.

"You people won't get rid of me that easily," he said as he departed.

Zakhar scowled alone at his desk, pondering the new sides of his Science Officer he had discovered.

What was the secret he and Sykora shared?

Was Javier staying a good thing or a bad thing? Was he starting to like being here, enough to hire on after he was free? Or was he waiting until he could see them all hang?

And what mind games would they start playing tomorrow?

READ MORE!

Be sure to pick up the other books in The Science Officer series!

The Science Officer
The Mind Field
The Gilded Cage
The Pleasure Dome
The Doomsday Vault
The Last Flagship
The Hammerfield Gambit
The Hammerfield Payoff

You can get volumes 1-4 collected together in
The Science Officer Omnibus 1

Volumes 5-8 are collected together in
The Science Officer Omnibus 2

Blaze Ward writes science fiction in the Alexandria Station universe (Jessica Keller, The Science Officer, The Story Road, etc.) as well as several other science fiction universes, such as Star Dragon, the Collective, and more. He also writes odd bits of high fantasy with swords and orcs. In addition, he is the Editor and Publisher of *Boundary Shock Quarterly Magazine*. You can find out more at his website www.blazeward.com, as well as Facebook, Goodreads, and other places.

Blaze's works are available as ebooks, paper, and audio, and can be found at a variety of online vendors (Kobo, Amazon, and others). His newsletter comes out quarterly, and you can also follow his blog on his website. He really enjoys interacting with fans, and looks forward to any and all questions—even ones about his books!

Never miss a release!
If you'd like to be notified of new releases, sign up for my newsletter.

I will never spam you or use your email for nefarious purposes. You can also unsubscribe at any time.

http://www.blazeward.com/newsletter/

Connect with Blaze!

Web: www.blazeward.com
Boundary Shock Quarterly (BSQ):
https://www.boundaryshockquarterly.com/

facebook.com/KRPBlaze

goodreads.com/Blaze_Ward

ABOUT KNOTTED ROAD PRESS

Knotted Road Press fiction specializes in dynamic writing set in mysterious, exotic locations.

Knotted Road Press non-fiction publishes autobiographies, business books, cookbooks, and how-to books with unique voices.

Knotted Road Press creates DRM-free ebooks as well as high-quality print books for readers around the world.

With authors in a variety of genres including literary, poetry, mystery, fantasy, and science fiction, Knotted Road Press has something for everyone.

Knotted Road Press
www.KnottedRoadPress.com